# Praise f

"Someone once asked
would there be enough

"*Kill All The Christians* goes to the very core of our
Christian faith. It challenges us to face the truth about why we
are Christians. It places our faith on center stage and demands
that we rid ourselves of fear and hypocrisy.

"Author Carolyn Franklin writes about the 'unthinkable'
taking place right here in an American Christian church. This
book will cause you to search your soul to find the grace of God
that will cause one to stand up with the Apostle Paul and
proclaim, 'For I am not ashamed of the gospel of Christ, for it is
the power of God unto salvation to everyone that believeth; to
the Jew first and also to the Greek.' (Romans 1:16-KJV)

"This book will both shock and bless you. Read it and
know that Christians in many other nations of the world are
suffering severe persecution. These shadows are right now
falling on America."

– Glynn M. Davis, Senior Pastor of Abundant Life Church,
Author of *They Shall Run and Be Weary* and
*The Power in The Blood*

"I couldn't put it down!"

– Dr. Denise Calloway/Maryland

"It's a wonderful fiction that takes us into the Western
Eurocentric church culture and the diverse fragile lives of saints
who attend with tiptoe faith in one hand and dice in the other!"

– Dr. Samuel Seward, Pastor of Living Faith
Community Church/Texas

"I especially enjoyed how the storyline and the dialogue of the
characters became alive throughout the pages… really engaging."

– Iris Powell/Texas

The Order Was Given...

# *KILL ALL THE CHRISTIANS!*

**CAROLYN E. FRANKLIN**

*Book Cover Design – Glynn Davis*

ISBN  0-7414-4978-1

**Published by:**

**INFINITY**
PUBLISHING.COM

*1094 New DeHaven Street, Suite 100*
*West Conshohocken, PA 19428-2713*
*Info@buybooksontheweb.com*
*www.buybooksontheweb.com*
*Toll-free  (877) BUY BOOK*
*Local Phone (610) 941-9999*
*Fax  (610) 941-9959*

**Printed in the United States of America**

**Printed on Recycled Paper**

**Published  January 2009**

## *Dedication*

*This book is dedicated to my earthly father, Emanuel Gulley (deceased) and my Uncle B. T., Booker T. Gulley (deceased) – Two who walked what they talked and through their lives the word of God was illuminated; and yes, the word of God still burn as fire shut up in my bones – Hallelujah!*

## *Acknowledgments*

Praises to the Father, my sweet Jesus, and the precious Holy Spirit who inspired and guided me through this writing.

My love, Tim, you are truly a man of God. Thank you for being the priest in our home. Thank you for making time to make me feel like I am the most beautiful woman in the world.

My precious children, born out of my heart (Josh, DeShone, and Amber), having you in my life gave me so very much to live for.

My gorgeous, precious mom, Dorothy, my Aunt Rosie, Aunt Mary, Aunt Ruth (deceased), and Aunt Lillie Mae; the singing and praying women in my life. You all are the epitome of the "True Mothers of the Church."

My sisters, Eva, Brenda, Deborah, Sharon, Adrianne, and Louise (deceased). My brothers, James, George, Micheal, Gregory, Emanuel (deceased), and Herbert (deceased). I am so glad our parents taught us about the Most High God and His love. I am blessed to be a part of siblings who know nothing but to love me, no matter what.

## *Special Acknowledgments*

My Father in the ministry, Pastor Glynn Davis and my beautiful Pastor Carolyn Davis…and God knew we would need you at such a time, at such a place when we needed you most. Thank you for being "real." Thank you for the encouragement and love you give so freely.

Pastor Samuel Seward and his beautiful wife, Vivian— you both are so very special to Tim and me. Thank you so much.

"And I will give you Pastors according to mine heart, which will feed you with knowledge and understanding." (Jeremiah 3:15)

# FOREWORD

Concentrated persecution and killing Christians is not surprising in places like Afghanistan, Iran, Pakistan, Saudi Arabia, Algeria, namely Muslim countries. Of course there are China, North Korea, Vietnam, India, and many others. Everyday in countries far away, Christians are persecuted and killed, because they are spreading the gospel (Matthew 24:14). In the United States, we don't endure the fear, pain, and suffering to the extent as Christians in other countries.

In "Kill all the Christians," you will experience what we truly can't fathom because we have religious freedom; it is a freedom that is so easily taken for granted. As a result, many who profess to be Christians do not value God or the Word of God as highly as Christians in countries with greater challenges.

This story serves to bring up close, what we feel is so far removed from us—making it tangible for the churches inundated with selfishness, materialistic concerns, position, status, acceptance by man; seeking man's approval rather than God's.

As more whispers are heard along with the Holy Spirit's, the sound of Satan has grown louder, but not stronger. And somehow many of our hearts have failed to comprehend the real treasure for we are looking through our own measure of substance. How can imperfect human beings truly capture the treasures given to us without the heart of Jesus Christ?

Nevertheless, Jesus' heart beats louder and stronger. As a result of these pages, perhaps, hearts will be convicted and began to beat with His as we re-evaluate ourselves, as we gather together in our "safe" sanctuaries.

"Suddenly, the door crashed open!  The sunrays glared purposely over the congregation.  Instinctively, members turned toward the entrance.  Pastor's look of composure was replaced with a frown.  The abrupt interruption of 'Praise God!' was the sarcastic, resounding voice of the tall, thin, white man with glasses as he proceeded down the aisle.  Part of the congregation's eyes traveled in calculated fashion as every step brought him closer.  Each 'Praise God!'  Still closer to the front. The other part of the congregation's eyes were fixed with indignation and caution on the other three visitors accompanying the tall man. A young woman and two other men.  They all held automatic rifles and revolvers...pointed at the parishioners."

# Kill all The Christians

The dawn began its sweep across the nation one Sunday morning. Many who displayed allegiance to the Christ stirred in their homes. Fathers, mothers, and children. Facets running, showers spraying. The sound of drawers and closet doors opening and shutting. Preparation for church has begun.

Kitchen utensils are heard as the coffee maker is prepared to start the coffee. Breakfast to be eaten. Cereal bowls with pouring milk. Bacon and sausages sizzling in skillets; eggs scrambled and fried.

One can hear the jingling of car keys as the members of various churches in the city get into their cars, vans, SUVs, and trucks with their families. Some filled with feelings of anticipation and some with feelings of obligation make their way to their respective churches.

As one takes the time to observe, there is a church of some sort on almost every corner. People are getting out of their vehicles to walk through entrances leading to a "holy" sanctuary.

This setting is displayed every Sunday. Many of these have been in church for many years. Then there are some who are relatively "new converts"-- ranging from a week to a year or so.

Preachers, teachers, evangelist, and exhorters are all spoken of in the Bible, along with the musicians, praisers, deacons, and ushers. Members of various congregations going to church as would be expected of Christians. Did not God give the Sabbath day as a day of rest for Christians? A day to rest in Him, His word. A day to spend in total worship and praise to Him.

So many are on their way to church with professions of Christ on their lips and through their attire, which includes hands and arms clutching bibles. The King James Version, New King James, New International Version (NIV), New Living Translation, Amplified... study bibles, parallel bibles. Engraved names on leather bounded covers. Some with simple paperback with words too hard to read because of the small print. Still in sincerity they carry it. After all, it makes an unsound yet profound statement, "I am a Christian. I believe in this book."

For those who find it unnecessary to grace the church with their presence, see the remote control in action. As they flip through the religious channels, they see some local churches. Hey! Mass on T.V! T. D. Jakes. There's that young man from Lakewood. Is that Joyce Myers? Well, how about that Juanita Bynum. Oh well, a Billy Graham or Oral Roberts' classic will do. Benny Hinn... the healer! They all talk about the Christ. Praise God!

Umm, and those who just do not bother at all to get up. Hey why bother? These are those who weigh the word of God with the action of God's people. These are those who watch us as we simply put God on and take Him off.

* * *

It's approximately ten o'clock a.m. at Mt. Sherman Community Church. Aah, the choir is in rare form as the singing voices reverberate against the walls. Acoustics are perfect as praise envelops the sanctuary. Congregational singing erupts. The momentum is ecstatic, electrifying as the director signals; the flow of the background comes in smoothly to intertwine into a single melodious squadron of worship and praise. Voices and instruments are all one.

Awesome! The words heard in refrain.

"Jesus, Jesus, you are our all!"

"Jesus, Jesus, you are our all and all!"

For those who are not quite sure of what to make of the astounding display of love in praise and worship to the King, they search their surroundings as though they are telescopes. They seek understanding with their eyes.

They see the twenty-seven year old mother's hands lifted, tears streaming down her face as she submits to the obvious presence of God. A few feet away, a robust, tailored-suited gentleman welcomes the release of the spirit. He is built like a NFL football player. He is such a tough looking guy, yet he is lifting his hands in total abandonment as are many others near him. One woman who looks to be in her late forties actually is dancing in the spirit, gazing above and beyond those who are present with her. She is clearly oblivious to everything except the One to whom she is displaying complete adoration.

The music's tempo wraps a bow of praise around those present. Anyone entering such a place at this moment cannot deny His existence.

The sweetness of such presence is profound and un-mistakenly felt by all present.

The minister walks to the podium; he humbly and serenely admonishes the people to take the opportunity to receive the gifts of God: salvation, a fresh anointing, even healing. He pauses in reverence as though his words are being measured out by the one for whom he is speaking. An orator of the Living God is wise to ponder as he speaks to God's people.

Such men and women of God are highly respected and are trusted. This pastor displays such carefulness... concerned with the truth.

A gleam-smiling usher helps direct a family—father, mother, nine-year old boy and ten-year old girl—to vacant seating. Hands extended to point to a place where they can be seated comfortably. She's faithful. Always ready to serve the people of God. Her welcoming smile holds no hint of

3

irritant as she moves up and down the aisles, available for questions and directions to assist. A servant indeed. The Pastor of the church knows her name and often uses her as an example of the faithful workers of the church. Always on time, always with a smile, never complaining. The epitome of servant-hood.

A couple of rows up sit several of the "mothers" of the church. Older women age 65 and above. Over the years it seemed to have become their section of the church. An unspoken mandate wholly accepted by the congregation as respect to the mothers of the church.

Mother Mary Johnson, the eighty-four year old widow of Deacon Leroy Johnson. What a long and fulfilled life they had shared. Children raised to know all about God. All finished college and self-sufficient. She sits smiling and nodding at the words of the minister. Three of her children: fifty-five year old Ryan, forty-two year old Sandra, and forty-five year old Theresa still attend and are very active in this church. The other two, Byron (fifty) and Pam (forty-nine), live out of state now but are active in the churches they attend.

She and some of the elders had worked for years in this church. It is one of the oldest churches in the city. Pride swelled in her chest as she surveyed the well-polished hardwood beams that held the ceilings. The chandeliers and lighting with grandeur so befitting for such a congregation who did not mind working for the Lord.

She remembered the pledges taken up over fifty years ago for the very foundation of this building. She and Leroy were one of the first families to place their check in the offering plate. Now just look at this place. Legs racked with arthritis made it difficult for her to walk, but she still made her way on Sundays. She still paid her tithes and offerings. (She uses a walker, which she places near the wall away from the congregation's pathway.)

4

Within these walls exist the peace of God. The unity of God the Father, God the Son, and God the Holy Spirit illuminates from the entrance to the choir loft, despite those counterfeited in their desire to be a part of such an unexplainable tranquility; those who had not yet given their lives to Christ.

To the naked eye, the "saved" can't be distinguished from the "unsaved." After all, church attendance is a plus in many circles. If you are not affiliated with some type of church, you are automatically considered a heathen. Heathens don't mix well in most communities with "church folks." Especially, when sought opportunities become available-networking.

*Let both grow together until the harvest: and in the time of harvest I will say to the reapers, gather ye together first the tares, and bind them in bundles to burn them: but gather the wheat into my barn. (Matthew 13:30—KJV)*

\* \* \*

Thirty–three year old Brenda Benson, Senior Resource Manager of Bronswell Incorporated, clapped her hands in sync with the choir as the "song of praise" sailed with a domino effect across the rows of parishioners—membership totaling four-hundred.

Brenda has been attending Mt. Sherman for almost two years now. Two of Bronswell's top executives also attended Mt. Sherman *(Bronswell is the largest logistic company in the Northern region of North America).* Brenda enjoyed good music. The musicians and songsters had truly gained her admiration. Their performances held an appeal that most can't resist. Almost like attending a free concert, Brenda reasoned.

Sure, Brenda recognized there is a Higher Being. Although for ulterior motives, coming here had exposed her to a point of view of spirituality that was somewhat intriguing. She even had concluded that history has a

5

connection with the Bible. She held a N.I.V. translated bible given as a gift by one of the missionaries of the church. Brenda's reading schedule was on Sundays, about this time when the Pastor or other ministers requested that all bibles be opened to certain scriptures for reading or reference. Nevertheless, on occasions she felt an "ah ha" moment. This served as a launch towards the true knowledge of God Almighty. There was just one problem. Brenda wasn't ready to give up on the treasures offered by the world.

Brenda was in love with Jerod Evans. Jerod was married with two children. Brenda and Jerod had been seeing each other for a year now. Ironically, she had met him at one of the church outings.

The Single Ministry was attending a bowling tournament. There were about twenty of them. Six guys and fourteen ladies. All with the sanctity cloud over their heads. All proper in manners modeled of Christians of a single ministry. Brenda had left the group to purchase a soda. Jerod was staring at her. She stared back. The opportunity for a brief moment to exchange names and numbers. Jerod's cell number of course. Brenda found out he was married two weeks after they started sleeping together. The titillating effect that was created with their union left no room for restraint. It was easier to conceal than to let go. With her own strength, she couldn't let go. She settled for the moments he would give her... no questions asked.

Minister Benjamin Perkins stood up to offer a prayer for the congregation.

"Heavenly Father!" he began. "I come as humbly as I know. Bless those present and those who are unable to be here.... "

Minister Perkins was one of the congregation's favorites. He knew what the church people wanted. He could manipulate their emotions if need be. His voice ranged from

6

a smooth, mild tone, to a roaring, bellowing, authoritative boom.

"We take authority over sickness, lack, poverty.... "

He could sense what they wanted to hear. He learned a long time ago to not be judgmental. Why bang God's people upside the head with reminding them of the Ten Commandments. After all, Jesus Christ died to save all. Why influx with condemnation. People needed to know the goodness of Jesus! People needed to keep holding on to the hope and peace of God!

Sometimes Minister Perkins became infuriated when the Pastor spoke against such matters as homosexuality, adultery, and the bottomless pit referred to as "Hell." People came to be uplifted not torn down with guilt. As a scholar, he reasoned, "There is no condemnation to those who are in Christ Jesus!" Besides, he had faults himself.

He occasionally went to the casinos, but he didn't consider it the worst thing he could do. He rarely spent a hundred bucks. It was a little recreation. He preached powerfully about the forgiveness of Jesus, but he still harbored resentment towards his ex-wife. She left him for another man. He had given her everything. All of his love, his money, everything! Even after five years, he hated her guts. He has to pay half of his paycheck for child support for his nine-year-old daughter, Sherry, whom he rarely gets to see because of his work schedule. He cringed at the idea of helping to pay for his ex-wife's and her husband's new, black Escalade. He still drove the 1995 Toyota Corolla they had during their marriage. No, he would not burden anyone else with the burden he carried. He would proclaim the goodness of Jesus!

"Father! We offer this petition to You, having faith that You will take care of Your children. We thank You now and we call it done. In the Name of Jesus! Amen."

The congregation refrained, "In the Name of Jesus!"

The choir director motioned to the choir and the resounding praise emerged as in agreement with what was asked of God:

"I've got a feeling everything is going to be alright!

I've got a feeling everything is going to be alright!

Be all right, Lord, be all right!"

Mrs. Helen Evans sat stoically, dressed in a beige tailor-made suit. One with explicit taste in fashion and etiquette, she was displeased with what she perceived as a deplorable display of emotions. "Why is it that people have to act like wild heathens?" she questioned. She failed to understand the changes that had infiltrated Mt. Sherman. Things use to be so much more structured and more orderly. She had been attending this church for twenty-five years. There was protocol worth resuming to keep the standards of God's church.

She averted her eyes as she noticed the young woman two seats ahead of her trying to get her attention. Last Sunday she'd appeased and nodded in recognition, but she couldn't act today. She had nothing for this young lady. She was so irritating. She and those four children of hers; she had heard they all had different fathers. This young lady was not married and probably hadn't completed high school. My goodness! Why doesn't she just turn around! Almost telepathically, the young girl turned back towards the choir, obviously disappointed.

\* \* \*

Joycelyn Williams, twenty-three years old with four children. She'd met Mrs. Evans one Saturday, three weeks before when Mt. Sherman had sponsored a street food ministry. Joycelyn and her children were staying with her disabled war veteran and ex-marine, Uncle Ben. He had lost one of his arms during the Vietnam War in 1965, shortly after President Johnson announced a major troop increase and bombing of North Vietnam.

They lived in a two-bedroom home three blocks away. Uncle Ben received a small disability check that barely covered the rent, not to mention his drinking habit. Joycelyn was so happy to see the tent and food set-up. Her food stamps had ran out, and she was going to have to go to the Red Cross the following Monday. She was helpless as to what she was going to do for food that weekend. A neighbor had mentioned to her that a church tent had been set up to feed the homeless and anyone hungry or in need.

Joycelyn had hurriedly tided up the kids ranging from ages two to eight years old. When they arrived at the tent, there was such a friendly atmosphere. The first person she had noticed was Mrs. Evans. Mrs. Evans was busily stirring pots and putting foods on plates. There were other members who assisted in getting beverages and seating families together to enjoy the meal. One lady with a big smile, the usher, invited Joycelyn to church service the next day. She also told Joycelyn that food would be served after services.

Joycelyn hadn't been to church since she was eleven years old. Her dad left her and her mom three days before Joycelyn's twelfth birthday. Her mom went into depression. She started drinking heavily. Her mother couldn't keep a job, so they had to move in with Uncle Ben. Joycelyn found herself at home alone most evenings after school. Her mom's constant drinking caused her to be in a perpetual stupor. Joycelyn's mother would go away on drinking binges weeks at a time. Many times when her mom made it home, she was usually too incoherent to notice Joycelyn, let alone care for Joycelyn. Uncle Ben spent most hours of the days and nights a few houses down the street, playing cards and drinking with another disabled veteran named Paul and his sister, Ernestine.

Joycelyn had to fend for herself. Eggs and ketchup were one of her favorite meals she had learned to cook.

Despite the conditions in which she lived, Joycelyn was a pretty bright student. She loved school. Her teachers always told her how smart she was. Joycelyn decided that one day she too would become a teacher or maybe a pediatrician.

One afternoon when she was fourteen years old, she was lying across the bed reading in the room she shared with her mother. She heard a noise at the front door. Thinking it was Uncle Ben, she continued reading.

Moments later she heard a slight noise. She glanced up and noticed that the doorknob to her room was turning slowly. In a moment, she realized something was wrong. It wasn't Uncle Ben at the door. It was Uncle Paul. She quickly sat up.

"Uncle Ben is not here. He.... "

Her voice seemed to be someone else's as she realized with horror that Uncle Paul's shirt was opened. His pants were also unbuckled. Moving towards Joycelyn, his eyes dark, mouth twisted, sickeningly slightly opened. Joycelyn remembers screaming, "No!" She hit at his face with her fist as he grabbed her arms and forced her on her back. Suddenly his full weight was upon her. Joycelyn struggled. Weeping. Screaming.

"Uncle Ben! Help me!" Paul held her down. With one hand he muffled her mouth. So rough and brittle.

Joycelyn smelled the stale alcohol. The stench was stifling as she willed herself to breath under his weight. Her pants were being pulled down; he ripped off her panties. Her muffled screams became a steady bawl as he assailed her innocence. She felt the rupturing of her insides. Each painful thrust tore into her soul. Slashing the very fiber of her spirit. She lost consciousness.

* * *

When Joycelyn awoke, hours later, she was in bed. She was covered. She cringed from the pain in her abdomen, her back, even her head as she sat up. She was wearing her nightshirt. She noticed a basin and towel near the bed. Her Uncle Ben was at the foot of the bed. His head in his hand. He looked up, wounded… eyes sad….

"I am sorry, Joy." His voice broke. His body shook as the tears of remorse showered from his eyes. He laid his head at the foot of the bed and cried repeating over and over again, "I'm so sorry!"

Joycelyn heard his words, but she could not comprehend them. She saw his tears, but she couldn't seem to connect them. She carefully turned away. She lay back down facing the wall. She closed her eyes willing herself the comfort of sleep… no sounds, but inside her head someone was screaming, "No!"

Joycelyn later learned that Uncle Ben lost the card game that afternoon. He had no money to pay but promised he would. Paul found another way to get paid.

The rape was never reported. Nine months later, Joycelyn gave birth to a baby girl. She never returned to school. The other three children, another little girl and two boys, were conceived during a common-law relationship. These children's father left before the birth of her youngest child. Between welfare and occasional part-time work, she was on her own. A few months earlier, she had to move back in with Uncle Ben.

Her mother? Somehow through the twists and turns of life, Joycelyn had no idea of the whereabouts of her mother. It seemed Uncle Ben had received information that she had been admitted to some state mental hospital.

Mt. Sherman had given her hope. Seeing Mrs. Evans, a very pretty, middle-aged woman busily cooking and serving meals made her heart swell with gratitude she couldn't explain. She was even more convinced that she and her children had entered a safe haven as the gleaming Usher escorted Joycelyn and her children to an area to sit and eat. For the first time in her life, she felt like she really mattered.

\* \* \*

The tall, white male in his late fifties ran his hands through his blond and gray streaked hair. His round framed glasses gave him a scholarly appearance—yet the troubled expression was more prominent. He checked his watch; it showed 11:00 a.m. He stood impatiently in his living room, surveying the scarcely furnished room. Two weeks after his wife of forty years, Dorothy, had lost the battle with breast cancer, he had placed the flower covered sofa and loveseat outside on the lawn, as a "free for all"—along with the sewing machine, coffee tables, and a couple of paintings. Too many memories. He closed his eyes. The pain seemed to grip his heart as the longing pierced through his being. He missed her so badly. As the pain surged and anger erupted, he hit the table in despair. Although his fist bore the brunt of the wood, he seemed oblivious to the pain.

He fought to erase the hideous, miserable sight of his once beautiful wife as she lay in bed writhing in pain. Sometimes howling out the name of Jesus. As she cried out helplessly, he too was helpless. What kind of God would allow such fate for such a gracious, beautiful woman? A woman who worked side by side with him in the orphanages, homeless, and abusive shelters. Giving of herself to so many. They both served Him in church as well as in their community. James Fieldman had a doctorate degree in Religious Studies. Yet with all of his learning, he did not know why his wife was held gripped in agony until death.

The sound of the tires on the gravel in the driveway halted the torture in his mind as he opened his eyes. He peered out the window. A black man, a shapely white woman with red hair, and a young almost goofy white guy. Reginald Garrett, Mae Sellers, and Cedric Mitchell. Mae held a cigarette puffing profusely. A sign of nervousness. He watched all three as they exited the 1980 model Ford van. They knocked. Fieldman opened the door. He did nothing to conceal his irritation.

"You are late!"

Quickly, Mae started, "We told Cedric.… "

Fieldman's glance in her direction caused her words to taper off.

"… but he.… " Mae clamped her lips shut.

Somehow Fieldman had a way of making her feel stupid. She resented this, but he was Reginald's friend. Reginald spoke up.

"James, we are here! We are still on schedule. As long as we leave at 11:30, we should be there before 12:00 as planned."

Reginald was Mae's boyfriend. They met in one of the local clubs six months ago. He was an ex-con—a title, Mae concluded, that didn't fit his personality.

Five years before, Reginald was a fifteen year vested employee who had worked his way up to a night-shift manager position. He was employed by one of the local distribution plants. He came home from work two hours early one night and found his wife in their bed with another man. In a raging fit of passion, he stabbed her lover several times with a seven-inch butcher knife. He proceeded to do the same to her, but she escaped to a neighbor's house. The police and an ambulance were called.

When the police officers arrived, he sat composed at his kitchen table. The knife lay on the table. He gave no resistance. He was handcuffed and taken into custody. He made the front-page news.

His wife's lover survived; he spent four months in the hospital and rehabilitation to recover from chest and abdomen stab wounds. Another stab wound was a severed nerve in his right arm, which caused a clot that left permanent damage to his right arm and leg. Reginald was charged with attempted murder and aggravated assault. He was sentenced to seven years in prison. Because of good behavior and no prior record, he served one year and was placed on parole. His wife wrote him letters while he was in prison. She stated she was sorry and had repented for her adultery. She also stated that she still loved him. Reginald never wrote back.

He tried to start over, but even with fifteen years of dedication on his job with an impeccable character record, his company felt it would adversely affect the reputation of the company for them to allow him to return. However, his employer did allow him to draw out his retirement fund, on which he was currently living.

Completing job applications was difficult. Every time he got to the part where it asked the question, "Have you ever committed a felony," he could not make himself write yes. He left a trail of incomplete job applications. A coldness grew in his heart.

Mae was a striptease dancer. A redhead. Straight up with no pretense. She said what she meant and meant what she said. Reginald found himself drawn to her daring approach to life. No counterfeit with Mae. You get exactly what you see. To the snobbish or self-righteous, she would be considered "improper." Reginald concluded that "improper" to some was like a breath of fresh air from those who pretended to be proper or noble. He and Mae held some things in common. They both were considered "undesirables." They both had a need to belong.

Fieldman opened a book he was holding. Writing on a note page inserted in the book, he then closed it and looked up.

"Let's go," he commanded.

As they exited the house, Cedric noticed a neatly folded paper near the step. Without much thought, he simply picked up the paper. Putting it in his pocket, he opened the van door and got in and sat on the back passenger side. Reginald was in the driver's seat. Fieldman sat in the front passenger side. Mae sat in the back behind Reginald.

The streets were clear. Not at all crowded as they normally are on weekdays. Strangely enough no one spoke. Reginald drove south on the freeway. Within twenty minutes, Reginald took the Carnival exit. They were headed to church.

* * *

The Pastor was standing behind the podium. "Please turn to 1 John 1:10."

Immediately, there is the rustling sound of turning pages. Gradually the sounds subsided as the people found the passage. Some unwilling to be noticed as unable to find the books of the bible, simply glanced at the page the bible fell on.

As was the custom, everyone stood and read the text along with the Pastor.

*"If we claim we have not sinned, we make him out to be a liar and his word has no place in our lives."*

The Pastor looked over the congregation motioning them to take their seats. His voice, though with expression of authority, was soothing as he addressed the congregation.

*"Proverb 3 states a liar is an abomination to God. Liars! Liars! Satan means Deceiver. Satan is the one who distracts you...whispering lies in your ear. He tells you wrong is right and right is wrong. We can find ourselves in sin yet refuse to recognize it as sin. Let's be real! As the world would say, 'Call a spade a spade!'"*

The small laughter could be heard among the congregation for such a cliché was unfounded in such a Pastor. He was almost monotonous. He wasn't the type to risk words; nevertheless, such a rarity in use of words allowed a moment of humor. He looked over the congregation. Almost thoughtful.

Suddenly, the doors crashed open! The sunrays glared purposely over the congregation. Instinctively, members turned toward the entrance. There stood four individuals with weapons drawn. Pastor's look of composure was replaced with a frown. The abrupt interruption of "Praise God!" was the sarcastic, resounding voice of the tall, thin, white man with glasses as he proceeded down the aisle. Part of the congregation's eyes traveled in calculated fashioned as every step brought him closer. Each "Praise God!" Still closer to the front. The other part of the congregation's eyes were fixed with indignation and caution on the other three visitors accompanying the tall man. A young woman and two other men. All held automatic rifles and revolvers…pointing at the parishioners.

"Bam!" The younger male quickly slammed the doors shut. Then the sound of 'click' as he secured the door. The sudden contrast of lighting seemed to have cloaked the sanctuary with an unpleasant dimness. Just as suddenly, a release of cries seemed to have ignited among the congregation.

"Oh, sweet Lord," several members began praying out loud. "Father in heaven…. God please hear us, Let God arise…. " Psalms began to be quoted. "The Lord is My Shepherd…. "

"Shut up!" The tall man with glasses growled. His voice laced with irritation. Some, undaunted, continued to pray aloud.

More menacingly and louder. "Shut up, you babbling, jabbering hypocrites!" He pointed a revolver towards several who were still praying out loud.

The second warning was effective. Prayer tapered off, quickly replaced by muffled cries and groans.

The black man walked briskly forward.

"Raise your hands."

Gun pointing as he motioned the rifle at the congregation.

"Now!" he warned, noticing several parishioners in shock as it slowly began to register that what was taking place was real.

Older saints who found it pleasant to just sit on Sundays with their hands on their laps, content with the understanding that they are older; justified complacency. Some had sung in the choirs faithfully or served on the usher board, even taught Sunday school for ten, twenty years before. They had earned the right to just sit with their arthritis and other ailments claimed. Nevertheless, today hands went up.

The redheaded lady walked up and down one aisle looking to make sure of cooperation. An older lady about the age of 80 struggled to lift her shaking hands. Too weak. She laid her palms on her purse.

"Why are you here?" The Pastor's voice, strangely calm. The tall man glared resentfully at the Pastor.

"To praise the Lord," he said sarcastically.

The Pastor, more forceful, "Why are you here?"

Angrily, the tall man rushed towards the Pastor. Several, obviously loyal deacons or committee members, instinctively started to step towards the tall gunman.

"Don't try it!"

Two of the other gunmen warned simultaneously. The black male and the young white male aimed the automatic rifles.

Two large men. one 350 pounds of muscles and the other no less than 300 pounds and approximately 20 years older, remarkably in shape. They stood near the gunmen, ready for an opportunity to disarm.

Brother Benny and his son, Bernard Smith. Both devout Christians. Both shared experiences in some of the most prestigious boxing rings in the country. So long ago.... Nevertheless, they often spent two to three days a week working out together at the local gym. Bernard's wife wasn't at church today. She was at home with their six-year-old flu-stricken son, Brian. Bernard praised God for their absence on this day. Mr. Benny had divorced Bernard's mom several years before. Before he had accepted Jesus as Lord. She attended church 20 miles from Mt. Sherman.

"Ah, well." The young male was circling the two masses as they stood, ready to project at any given second. The young man reached inside the pocket of his jacket and pulled out a snubnose revolver and placed it at the base of Mr. Benny's neck.

Mr. Benny, fearless. He wore a slight grin, which was almost eerie under the circumstances.

"Use it, but I'll still be living." Smooth, composed.

Bernard knew his father well. Mr. Benny loved Jesus. He had no reasons to fear—he knew where he'd be.

"You, on the other hand, need Jesus."

The young man struck Brother Benny's temporal with the butt of the revolver. Mr. Benny fell to his knees. A crimson flow ran down his face. He did not cry out; he did not make a sound to indicate pain. Instinctively, Bernard reached towards his father.

"I'm all right, son." Mr. Benny managed to lift his head, his eyes meeting his son's. Assurance on his face. "All is well," he managed, though lightly.

"Boom!" Two shots fired into the sanctuary. Screams. People hit the floor cowering. The tall man was holding the gun threateningly.

"One more move and you all die. Starting with your Pastor." The tall man's voice was cold.

"Then you, old man." The young man snarled, looking down at Brother Benny. The gun at his head. Bernard's massive chest moved rapidly as every part of his being sought to burst through with a fury he hadn't felt since his last boxing match, nine years before. His father's eyes bored into his son's. Brother Bernard read the message. He nodded his head slightly to acknowledge that he understood. "The time will come. Allow God to orchestrate." The young man could not see the communication.

The tall man motioned to the mother section of the sanctuary. Several of the elderly women looked at each other with wonderment on their faces. The redhead walked up to the tall man and he gave her instructions. Not sure, the mothers sat and watched. The redhead, almost apologetically stood near the area. A mandate.

"You all get up and come with me." Several of the older ladies began to stand up.

One gray-headed old lady spoke up.

"Young lady, we can't all walk."

She nodded at several walkers and wheelchairs that were in a corner nearby.

Clearly frustrated, Mae retorted, "Just whoever can walk, get over here!"

The old lady with three others remained seated. The young lady warned them.

"Any attempt to do anything other than walk and I will shoot."

A hush went over the congregation at the threat towards the older women. Several voices called out, "Mom please just do as she says."

"Granny!" A young girl, around the age of twelve, screeched.

A thin, light-skinned woman; she looked to be in her early seventies with gray-black hair turned towards her granddaughter. Tears crested her cheeks. She held a handkerchief to her lips to stifle a cry. She motioned with her finger, "Shush" to the young girl. She went with the other women.

One of the members placed an arm around the girl to comfort her, whispering, "She'll be all right."

Sons, daughters, and husbands stood helplessly as the elderly women were led away.

"Get down here with your people, Pastor!" The tall man ordered sarcastically.

The Pastor, head up and observing as he walked two steps down. He was on the flooring with the people. The tall man went up and stood behind the pulpit.

"All women with infants and toddler children come to the front. Sit here." He pointed to the area where the elderly women had been. Several women began moving, holding their babies…fear escalating with every minute, with every order given.

"Don't make me persuade you." The tall man noticed one of the women hesitating.

The mothers gathered bags, purses, etc.; husbands and wives with newborns hugged as they parted, strengthening one another. Single moms obeying as they held babies close… moving in the direction given.

Joycelyn's eyes watered—trying to hold the threatening flow as she shushed her eight year old daughter who started to go with Joycelyn, who shook her head from side to side to gesture "No."

"Hell is everywhere for me!" Her thoughts. She held her youngest as the other two children walked with her. She saw the smiling usher. Only she was not smiling. Her face distorted in totally disbelief at what was taking place. The usher had clutched papers in her hands. Nervous, unsure.

"Without the smile, she looks like me." Joycelyn did not understand why such thoughts entered her mind. She and the other moms followed as ordered. She observed the calmness of the Pastor. "I wonder if he is as scared as I am."

The Pastor's eyes never left the tall man except to check the places of the other gunmen. His thoughts unreadable. Silent. Not even flustered. Silent.

The tall man turned the pages of the Pastor's written notes. The gunman, sardonic, scowling, turning the pages of the book.

"A liar. Yes, this is true. You are a liar." He was speaking to the congregation. "Look at yourselves."

All eyes bored towards this man. Many who eyed him prayed that God would send help.

There were a few whose state of fear left them paralyzed in thoughts that weren't clear and incoherent of anything but the gunmen holding them hostage in church. Then there was the handful that knew that Satan controlled these gunmen. Satan had orchestrated this. They prayed that God would begin work through their hearts and minds. That these gunmen would know Jesus through this.

The tall man glared across the sanctuary. "Christians, you say you are! Ok, Christians. This is your day! Today is the day we kill all the Christians!"

* * *

The fear masking their faces turned to pure terror as the people listened to the plans set by these gunmen.

"No!" A woman screeched—Mrs. Evans. She fainted. Those close by struggled to allow her to lie on the full length of the pew.

The young gunman looked puzzled. Although unsure, he quickly regained his composure. Wow! He'd been told they'd rob the good church folks and leave. What was this? Oh, he reasoned, Fieldman was just dubbing up. He smiled as he realized the effect of Fieldsman's statement, "Kill all the Christians! Yeh!"

Brenda felt her knees shaking uncontrollably. She heard herself speak—shocked by her voice.

"What…sir…what do you mean by Christians?" Her tongue seemed so heavy…breathing caused her to stammer.

"I mean...I…," Brenda searched for words. "I haven't been attending church long!"

Fieldman roused backwards and released a bellowing laugh.

"A Christian? You do not know what a Christian is? Ain't all y'all a Christian?"

He laughed. Then just as abruptly stopped. Frowning with distain as his eyes traveled across the sanctuary.

"I will give you all a chance to decide. Christians, move to the right of the church. If you are not a Christian, stay where you are."

The Pastor, without hesitation, walked to the right of the church, as did half of the parishioners. Rev. Perkins stepped over towards the Pastor—Unsettled, yet knowing the right thing to do. A third of the choir members walked down the platform to the right. Several women reached out to help

Mrs. Evans as she had gradually regained consciousness. She waved them on shaking her head.

"I can't move. Go on." They left her. Mrs. Evan evaded their eyes as she sat passively taut.

The black gunman stared at the remaining parishioners.

"This is interesting. Hey!" He turned to the tall man. "I thought everybody who go to church were Christians."

The tall man smiled as though satisfied that these who disclaimed Christianity were the validity to the hypocrisy of Christianity.

The usher stood stoic, nervous. She had not walked over with her Pastor. Her mind was far from the approval of anyone. Nevertheless, she felt some regret at having not moved with the other Christians. "God forgive me." She repeated over and over in her mind. "Please forgive me."

Brenda had taken a step with several of the members moving to the other side, but somehow she decided, "This is between them and the Christians. Not me. I haven't told any of these people I was a Christian." Interestingly enough, one of the executives from the firm where she worked also made no move. She pacified herself with this thought.

*Whosoever shall deny me before men, I will deny before my father, which is in heaven, (Matthew 10-33—KJV)*

The redhead had returned to the sanctuary with a ring of keys in her hands.

"Look what I have. I locked those old hens in one of the rooms."

The young man smiled approvingly.

"Good. We can deal with them later."

Brother Bernard had helped his father over to the right side of the church. Someone had handed him several handkerchiefs. Two were tied together and made as one to tie around his head where he had been hit. Blood soiled through a bit, but the bleeding had stopped.

* * *

Outside Mt. Sherman, the sunshine was radiant. It was a beautiful Sunday. Cars passed by going to other churches. With doors closed and stained glassed windows, no one could have guessed what was taking place. Unless....

A gray impala turned into the parking lot. Thirty-four year old Paul Richardson quickly parked. He turned off the ignition. Hastily grabbing his bible and suit coat, he rushed up the steps to get to service. Unusually late, he pulled the door handle.

"Um?" Locked.

"No." He pulled again several times.

"Is the door stuck?" He thought.

"Why isn't it opening? Where are the ushers? Especially.... "

For a moment he smiled, relishing the thought of seeing her. That smile.

"Now this is ridiculous. Why would the front doors be locked?" Strange.

He walked quickly to the back door. No entrance. Then to the side door which was also locked. Paul knew that this was normal; it was precautionary to keep the back and side doors locked due to the increased crime in the community. Maybe one of the windows? He quickly dismissed this idea. They are stained glass windows, for God's sake. He couldn't see through them anyway. He shook his head for having thought of such a stupid idea.

"What?" Paul was puzzle.

He surveyed the parking area. He noted the parked cars, trucks, SUV's—even a raggedy van near the front entrance.

"Now, why did someone park near the front entrance anyway? That is not a parking place." He studied the premises.

"This is crazy!" He walked back to the front door and literally knocked on the door.

Inside, the parishioners glanced hopefully at the door.

Help! God has sent help! Initial thought.

The tall man waved to the young man who stood near the entrance. Revolver in place, ready to pull the trigger.

"If we scream," one woman thought. "That would let them know."

"Help us!" Someone else was thinking the same thing. A young man in his early twenties. One of the Christians.

The tall man grabbed a one-year old little girl off the lap of her mother. The baby began to cry from his bruteness. He held a pistol to her head.

The baby's mother screamed and begged, "Please don't, please!"

"Cry for help again and this child dies first."

The young man's eyes were wide in horror. Fieldman's eyes were dark and ominous as he stared at the young man.

"I'm sorry. Please, sir! I am so sorry!" he pleaded. "I won't do it again. Please!"

The mother sobbed, "No!"

The baby wailed.

* * *

Outside with cars passing, Paul could hear nothing. Mt. Sherman's doors were thick and strong. He knew nothing of what lay on the other side of the doors of Mt. Sherman. Yet, he knew all was not well. He went to his car. He sat. He began to pray, unsure of what else to do.

The tall man stepped closer to the young man. Snarling under his breath; the young baby was sniffling now. Tears spent. She eyed Fieldman, the young man, then she turned seeking her mother.

"God forgive me!" the young man cried.

The tall man leaned over. His hot breath smelled of coffee.

"You are a pansy aren't you?"

The young man looked at Fieldman.

"What is your name?" The tall man demanded. The gun still pointed at the baby.

"Craig." His voice trembled. He was the youth minister of music.

"Craig," the tall man echoed.

"Only a pansy would scream out like you did. You sorry excuse for a man."

He gradually lowered the gun. But just as suddenly he raised it again. Pointing it squarely between Craig's eyes.

Craig felt the coldness of the pistol. Hard. Somehow in his mind, he imagined that the barrel was hot as well as cold.

The one-year old looked. Without taking his eyes off of Craig, the man lowered the baby down out of his arms. The baby at the early stages of walking stood then turned as she heard her mother whisper.

"Come Lillie."

Sniffling, the baby walked awkwardly towards her mother. Falling…getting on all fours, then standing… testing her balance again. Standing and holding to the seat. The mother quietly moved closer crouching to pick her up. Sobbing she held her close. The mother hurried to return to where she was sitting.

The tall man's attention was squarely on Craig. Craig's eyes were closed. Breathing fast. Shaking.

"Pansy, Pansy," the man taunted.

"You have never been with a woman have you, Craig?"

Craig's lips trembled.

"No." He replied softly.

"What?" The man urged him.

"No!" Craig sounded louder.

"Why?"

Craig's eyes still closed.

"I will blow your sorry hairs off of your head. Answer me, Pansy!" Angrily, hot.

"I don't know!" Craig trembled.

"Oh, you don't? I'll tell you why! Because you are a faggot! A homosexual, gay, flaming faggot!"

Craig shook. Tears seeped through his closed eyes. He had never felt so hopeless, so exposed, so vulnerable. He knew what he was although he hid it as much as he could.

The man pushed him against the pew roughly. Craig fell against the back of the pew. His eyes opened only slightly as he reached his arms back to break his fall. The tears, the pain. What he was multiplied by this announcement. He sank in defeat against the pew. He rolled into the fetal position and wept uncontrollably.

The tall man was satisfied for now. He turned and walked back towards the front of the church.

* * *

The black gunman scanned the church. Several of the women reminded him of Lisa, his ex-wife. They all looked the same—all holy with little secrets too big to keep. He wondered.

She used to make him attend church sometimes. There were times he felt that he was getting somewhere. There was something to church after all. He had on occasion looked forward to church. Nightshift demanded overtime that made it difficult to maintain consistency in attending services. And then to come home and find his wife and another man, this wiped out any connections he thought he had with God.

Mrs. Evans sat unsure of what to do. She looked and listened to all that was taking place.

"The neighborhood," she thought.

"How did we get to this?" She sat incredulous to all that was taking place.

"In my own church. America! Why isn't someone knocking the door down to rescue them? Where is the police?"

"Christians make me sick!" His voice held distain.

The tall man had returned to the pulpit. He scrutinized the sanctuary. Anger shrouded his face as he loathed each one. He seemed to be waiting for a response. All eyes were locked on the troubled man. His hate illuminated towards the people; the demonic hate for the people of God.

"You!" He pointed at an elderly man on the right side of the church. The elderly man was stocky, in his early seventies.

28

"How long have you been a Christian?"

The man, unsure, looked to his left and right making sure it was he who was being addressed. The man stood up.

"I've been a member of this church near fifty years…."

Bam! The thunderous sound of the stand as it toppled over. Mouths across the congregation gaped with surprise. Fieldman had pushed the podium over, enraged at the response.

"A member? Oh, I see. A member!"

"I…I was baptized at twenty, so it would be forty-seven years I've been a Christian," the man hurriedly clarified. His face wore a frown of frustration. He licked his lips nervously. Why was his mouth so dry?

"Forty-seven glorious years!" Fieldman mocked. "Tell me. Have you ever met me before today?"

The elderly man slowly shook his head "No," not sure of what response the gunman was seeking.

"Oh, yes you have! All of you have. I'm the one who needed, no, craved to understand the illustrious Christians. Yes, because your membership held me at bay… I have to love this Jesus."

The man cut in.

"Sir, I have not…. " The man's words faltered.

Steel-eyed, the tall man's voice cracked like a whip in the acoustics of the sanctuary.

"You! Many like you! Too many like you! Almost like a disease you brag on this Jesus!" Fieldman ranted.

The tall man frowned. He suddenly stopped speaking.

"The name of Jesus." His voice had suddenly become a whisper.

"The name…. " He seemed to have suddenly thought of something. The room was silent. His knees seemed to buckle. Fieldman wrestled.

"Dorothy."

Brother Bernard was calculating as he noted the stressed man. If he could just get close, he could overpower him and perhaps use him as negotiation to free the others. He watched.

Fieldman seemed to have become disoriented. Reginald was perturbed at the tall man's display. He pointed the gun menacingly at the parishioners, as he moved closer to Fieldman. Sensing his movement, the tall man began to regain his composure.

Suddenly, Bernard leaped towards the gunmen. The full force of his body landed squarely on Fieldman. Several of the members rushed Reginald. Simultaneously a gunshot fired.

"Bang!" Glass shattered.

"Ugh!" a man yowled in pain as he was hit by a bullet. Everyone froze.

A man had Reginald in a headlock and another was trying to take his gun. When the shot rang, everyone stopped.

Blood was on the floor. The tall man and Bernard were still on the floor, blood underneath their bodies. The tall man moved. Pushing Bernard's body away, Fieldman sat up stunned but still holding his revolver.

The young gunman had fired the shot. His eyes were wide almost frightened, not sure of what he'd done.

"I had to shoot him!"

By now Reginald had managed to wrestle out of the grip of the man who held him. He held the gun pointing and ready to shoot.

Brother Benny was restrained by several members as his son lay on the floor unconscious.

"Oh my God!"

Brother Benny, the Pastor and some of the other members began to pray.

"Call an ambulance! Please!" an older woman, Mrs. Johnson lamented.

"Please at least call an ambulance."

"I am a doctor." A voice three rows behind her.

"Please allow me to check him."

The tall man—now standing—motioned to Reginald and nodded his head in the direction of Bernard. Reginald scowled at the doctor. "Go on!"

The forty-two year old doctor went and knelt next to Bernard. He checked his pulse. Then, he placed his head on Bernard's chest. He checked the area of the gunshot. The blood seeped through the white shirt, the right side. He opened the shirt.

"He's dying. I need to move him."

"He will just be the first one to die!" the tall man retorted.

"After all, he is a Christian!"

Mother Johnson chirped in, "No, this is not the way!"

Eyes turned to the old mother. Unable to walk, she was one of the three mothers who were left in the sanctuary when the other mothers were marched out. She turned to Fieldman.

"You are a disgraceful man. I've seen you somewhere before. I just can't seem to recall."

She moved her hands across her forehead as though it would help with her memory.

"Why do you want us dead?"

Fieldman stared coldly at the woman. "Because...."
He paused and slowly continued. "It is all a lie. Your lies
have done nothing but build a religion for comfort. Comfort
at the expense of broken promises and dreams. You have
fathomed a God to excuse you for everything, to give you
everything. I am God today! After being given everything,
what is left but death?"

Mrs. Johnson gasped and held her face in her hands
as she cried.

Fieldman howled with laughter, amused by the effect
he had on the woman. He was beyond tears.

* * *

The mothers of the church had followed the orders of
the redheaded young lady. She had led them out of the main
sanctuary and down a hall. She ordered them into one of the
classrooms normally used for morning Sunday School
classes. It consisted of several tables with folding chairs.

"Why did you come here, young lady?" The small
voice of one of the mothers.

"Don't ask me any questions. Do as you are told,"
Mae ordered.

Mae had surveyed the room as they obediently seated
themselves at the tables. No struggles, silent. She noticed
that several had tears that ran down their faces. Quietly a
handkerchief would pass from one to another. For the most
part, these women were... Mae's heart began to beat faster at
a sudden flashback. Mama Foster would have been around
the same age as these ladies. Mama Foster/aka Mama Mimi.
Something caught in her throat. She coughed. Holding her
hand over her mouth. Gun still pointed towards the mothers,
she cleared her throat. Shakened.

"If you try anything, I'll kill you, ok?"

The mothers looked at the young lady. Pity seemed to be the consensus as they sat. Several mothers started opening their bibles, laying them on the table where they sat.

Mae noticed a ring of keys on the shelf near the door of the room. She grabbed them hastily. She felt an urge to run. She quickly stepped on the outside of the room and abruptly closed the door. Her hands shook as she tried each key to the door. Third try, yes! She locked the door.

"Now, they can't get out." Her emotions were fighting against the realization that it wasn't as important to lock the old women in the room as it was to get out of that room. That place where the old women were opening the Bible. In the room she felt something she did not understand.

A songster—one of the mothers started singing.

"Hum, just another day that the Lord, has kept me!

Hum , just another day…."

Mae glanced at the door as she backed away from the sound of the mothers singing…was it singing? Or was it moaning, groaning? The sound seemed to penetrate… seeping through the locked door. Mae turned and practically ran back to the main sanctuary. When she made it to the sanctuary, she held the keys like a trophy. She was still in control she told herself.

Several of the mothers, including the tall thin mother, did not have a bible nor did they sing. Their thoughts were entrapped with all that was taking place.

The strong voice of the leading songster continued.

"Just another day that the Lord has kept me!"

The song seemed to give strength as a reminder of the well-known scripture in Nehemiah,

*"The joy of the Lord is my strength."* (Nehemiah 8:10—KJV)

Something so serene in such dismal circumstances. *"And Paul and Silas...they sang hymns and prayed and the doors were opened..."(Acts 16:25-26—KJV)*

Mrs. Rosie, one of the mothers, took off her glasses to wipe off a seemingly light film. She replaced them. The film was still there. She removed her glasses again. She wiped and replaced the glasses. She looked up. It looked as though there was more film. Suddenly, she realized just as the Holy Spirit whispered and as she spoke aloud,

"Isaiah 6 states, '*And the Glory of the Lord filled the temple....*'"

This was no film on her glasses. This was the glory of the living God in this place. The convictions of all hearts present began to beat as one in happiness as they realized the miraculous presence. Something was taking place. Everyone began to sing. Tears began to flow in the comfort of the Holy Spirit.

\* \* \*

Bernard lay on the floor regaining consciousness. He heard voices. He felt a sharp pain on his right side. His fingers felt the thickening of blood. He remembered moving towards the tall man, the sudden jolt and the sound of gunshot. The bullet had gashed straight through... a searing flesh wound.

"Get that heap out of here!" Fieldman ordered the doctor and another man.

Reginald pointed his gun towards them. One got his arms, the other his feet. They more or less dragged his body towards the room nearby. The choir room.

Brother Benny was weeping as several of the members cautioned him.

"Losing your life will not bring Bernard back... he wouldn't want you to be hurt." Brother Benny talked to God as he wept.

Bernard had lain rigidly as Dr. Nelson had opened his shirt, feeling for a bullet entry. The doctor noted that no bullet was lodged. He did not display any sign of a prognosis. Standing in the doorway with a gun pointed in their direction, Reginald allowed them to place Bernard's body on the sofa. So much blood. However, Bernard was strong, healthy. The doctor grabbed a nearby scarf and quickly tied it around Bernard's waist, putting pressure on the wound. The doctor and the other man walked back out of the room. Reginald observed the blood. Yes, he was as good as dead. Reginald closed the door firmly behind them.

* * *

Bernard opened his eyes. The throbbing pain in his side was almost unbearable. He had fought the urge to cry out as they moved him. He moved to sit up. Holding his side, he applied more pressure. He thought of the first aid kits that were included in every ministry room in the church. He braced himself. He managed to stand. He prayed.

"Father, give me the strength, help me to stop the blood; cover me and replenish me with the blood of your son Jesus. In Jesus name Amen."

He managed to walk several steps to the nearby shelf. He pulled the door opened. There were towels, peroxide and bandages. He opened the bottle. He loosened the scarf. He put one towel in his mouth, biting down. He leaned to his left. Pouring the peroxide, he muffled the roar that threatened to come through. Raw flesh. He placed a towel underneath the scarf. He tightened... pressure.

He looked down and noticed he had made a blood trail from his movements. He poured some of the peroxide on the towel, then put the towel on the floor and used his feet to dry up the trail, moving his feet back and forth. He made it back to the sofa. He pushed the soiled towel underneath the sofa. He lay back down. He needed to rest.

He felt himself losing consciousness. Somehow, he felt he was not alone. The need for sleep registered in his mind. He became acutely aware of a deep sense of peace; he savored this sweetness, eyes closed... he drifted off.

* * *

Outside in the parking lot, Paul thought he'd heard gunshots. Paul looked up, shocked by the shattering pieces of one of the stain-glassed windows.

"Ok, this is crazy!"

He picked up his cell, dialed 911 and began speaking rapidly. He relayed the abnormalities... and the shots... sounded like a gun shot... then the shattering stain-glassed window.

Inside, James Fieldman's mind was filled with evil thoughts..."Kill, destroy them...," reprobated in every sense.

His accomplices were all ignorant to his true plans. Sure he wished to prove the fraudulent religion. It was important to show the fallacy of this country's foundation. A Christian country founded under God. What God? A country quick to ridicule, seeking to reduce the validity of religions of other countries—especially the Muslim countries.

"Islam the devils, hum!"

Fieldman understood the persecution of the Christians and the missionaries that poured in like locust in various nations, which had no connection with Christianity. He had been one of them. He and his precious wife, Dorothy, toiled in their mission to spread the Gospel. Their Presbyterian affiliations had frequently sought out missionaries.

His sweet Dorothy. It was through her urging that he furthered his studies in religion. There was nothing he would not do for her; everything he pursued was through her love. Sure he learned about God and yes, he learned prayers to God; but the love he shared with Dorothy could not be shared with a God he had not truly met. Yet he had served as a Presbyterian missionary.

*"No none can serve two masters. For you will hate one and love the other; or be devoted to one and despise the other." (Matthew 6:24--KJV)*

How lost he truly was without Dorothy. He wanted to inflict the pain in his heart on these lying crooked people. He will carry out his own execution today.

\* \* \*

A couple of weeks before, Fieldman had searched through the phone book to choose this spot. No method just simply a church. Mt. Sherman caught his attention. He had written a note and even included his return address. It stated, "I will visit soon." In essence he was letting them know he was coming. He mused at the conclusion that to the church, he would be just another fool to put money in their offering plate.

Strangely enough, around this same period, Pastor had a dream:

He saw two men fishing near the shore of an ocean. As he watched, one of the men had a large bowl filled with fresh water in which to clean his fish. The other did not. Both men were successful in catching fish. The men cooked their fish and ate of it.

A voice asked, "What was the purpose of the fish?

Pastor answered, "The men were hungry. The purpose of the fish was for them to eat."

The voice asked, "Was the purpose fulfilled?"

"Yes," Pastor replied.

"No." the voice corrected.

"As each man ate, their flesh hunger was satisfied; but as for the one who ate the unwashed fish, in his very bowls lay a bacteria that will multiply into an infection that will weaken this man then he will die.

The fish must be washed. Catching the fish has become an art. The cleaning is lacking. Unclean fish will appear to serve its purpose, but ultimately the bacteria will manifest into a form of weakness, sickness, then death. Man of God, the fish must be washed."

Pastor woke up. He lay awake for hours pondering the dream before finally returning to sleep.

Pastor was in his office the next day when a letter arrived. The envelope had a return address but no name. He read the letter. "I will visit soon." There was nothing more. Somewhat perplexed, on the following day, the pastor made a visit to the address on the envelope. It was in a neighborhood about twenty minutes from Mt. Sherman. He came to a small, framed three-bedroom house—white with yellow shutters. The grass was unkempt, yet there was the noticeable array of red and yellow roses that peeked between the overgrown grass. He knocked on the door. No answer. He waited a few moments then knocked again, harder. No one answered. The pastor reached into his coat pocket and pulled out a note pad. He wrote a message and signed it...

"... *Pastor, Mt. Sherman Community Church.*"

He folded the paper and opened the screen door, closing it on the paper to hold the note in place.

* * *

Jerod had been waiting at his mother's for 30 minutes. His wife and children sat watching television in the family area. They were going out to eat Sunday dinner.

Normally she would be here by now, he thought. He could almost see his mom's brisk walk towards the exit after the sermon. She never waited around any longer than she had to after church.

Jerod and his family were not regular attendees of Mt. Sherman. Of course, every once in a while, on special occasions such as Mother's Day, Easter and Christmas, they have gallantly made their way to represent "family." It had been over a year since they had visited. Maybe next Sunday, he considered as he glanced at his wife sitting with the children.

Jerod and Christina had been married ten years now. He worked at a computer company. He did very well as part of their top resource personnel. Christina was a stay at home mom since the birth of little Gerald, now two years old. Jerod Jr., the oldest, was four years old. Daycare was expensive; he and Christina decided it would be better financially for her to quit her secretary position at the legal firm where she worked. Staying at home also proved beneficial in caring for the boys, giving them the attention they would not receive in a daycare with other children.

Little Gerald was looking up and smiling at his mother, reaching out both arms to be hugged. She smiled and pulled his little frame closer. He snuggled contently. Jerod Jr., not wanting to be left out, leaned on his mother's arm. She used her free arm to wrap him close.

Jerod seized the moment, rating the appreciation he felt towards his wife, as a mother, a homemaker, and a friend. If only....

He began the debate in his mind, for what could have been the "thousandth time," his reasons for infidelity. Jerod had needs. He needed a lover. Christina's life was so consumed with the boys. He just didn't get those intimate moments he craved. He'd had a couple affairs over the years. There was a time he felt ashamed of his unfaithfulness.

Ultimately he justified his adultery through his commitment to his family. He had no intentions of leaving his wife and kids for anyone. Nevertheless, to quench the fierce fire within him, he must have the delectable warmth of an uninhibited woman. His mind began to reflect on last night.

* * *

Brenda was always available to serve his needs. He used the excuse of visiting his mother countless times to spend hours of almost insatiable lovemaking. They never talked about their personal lives. Their moments were solely about each other. As a married man who has so much to lose, an affair is precarious. Yet, he could see no way out. A dilemma? Yes, but for now, a necessary one.

His cell phone rang, interrupting his thoughts. It was his brother, Jonathan.

"Hello."

"Jerod. Man, turn on the T.V. Where are you man?"

The sound of his brother's voice immediately disturbed Jerod.

"I'm at Mom's. We are suppose...." Jonathan broke in.

"Man, turn to the news. Hurry!"

"All right, Ok!" Jerod was now alarmed.

"Christina, turn the television to a news channel!"

Christina heard the urgency in his voice. A questioning look formed on her face as she obeyed his instructions. She picked up the remote control from the coffee table and quickly turned to a local news channel.

On the T.V. screen, Mt. Sherman was being shown. A reporter was stating, "...gunman?" She turned up the volume.

"Apparently the members of Mt. Sherman are being held as hostages. No details on the gunman or how many gunmen there really are. It is clear that they are armed and dangerous." A lady reporter was speaking.

Police cars were lined up. Officers surrounded the church, armed and waiting. There was a young man dressed in slacks, shirt and tie speaking with several officers. One of them was writing as he spoke.

The reporter continued, "The authorities are unable to divulge anymore information for fear of the parishioners' safety. It seems that no apparent demands have been made. No plans to what the gunman or gunmen have for the members. The authorities have assured the public that they are using the maximum of precaution to defuse the situation. This is Cathy Staggard reporting live at WALX, News Channel 43."

Jerod's heart was pounding. Jonathan was almost hysterical.

"Man, Mama's in there! What are we going to do? What can we do?"

"Look Jonathan, I'm headed to the church. Meet me there."

Jonathan's voice cracked, "Ok, man. Ok!"

Jerod hung up his cell phone, thrusting it in his pocket. Christina's eyes locked with his. The fear was evident.

"Jerod, please be careful!"

Jerod hugged her and the boys, told her to lock up the house and for them to meet him at their home later. Fortunately, his mom had a small car in the garage. He took its key from the key shelf near the fireplace and rushed out to the car. He hadn't had a reason to talk to God in a long time. He wondered if God would hear him now.

The church office was near the sanctuary. The phone began to ring.

Ring!

Fieldman knew that the gunshots made earlier had more than likely been heard by the nearby residents. Also, whoever came to the door and found it locked would have found it strange. Fieldman nodded to Reginald and the young gunman for them to keep their guns on the congregation. Fieldman walked over to the church office, he opened the glass door. He picked up the phone on the desk near the door.

"Yes!" Fieldman's voice drawled with impatience at the disturbance.

"This is Leutinant Karl Inwood with the 15$^{th}$ Precinct of Newark. Who am I speaking with?"

Fieldman chuckled menacingly and said, "Leutinant Inwood, we are having church. Don't call anymore, unless you want me to start shooting. We will call you!"

He slammed the phone on the receiver, then as an afterthought, he snatched the telephone cord out of the phone jack. Suddenly, the phone soared across the room and crashed against the wall. Fieldman's face was set with an unrelenting determination.

"I loathe the Cavalry of every kind."

\* \* \*

The policemen had Carnival Avenue off limits. Cut off. No one could enter nor leave within a two-mile radius without permission from the authorities. It was now mid-afternoon, at approximately 2:30 p.m. People had gathered outside. Family members and friends stood outside; some neighbors sat on their lawns and on their porches. Faces of disbelief, heads shaking, as many tried to make sense of what was really taken place. Waiting for an explanation.

Paul Richardson was sitting in one of the patrol cars. The police force had responded pretty quickly. He'd repeated everything he had told the 911 Operator. He listened to the officers as they talked among themselves. His church family was in trouble. All he could do was pray.

"Hey, man. Here's a burger and soda." Sergeant Stephens, a twenty-year veteran on the force. It had been close to two hours since the initial contact with the gunman. Paul accepted the food. He'd been in too much of a hurry to eat breakfast.

"Thanks," Paul said.

Sergeant Stephens patted Paul on the shoulder and turned back to speak with the officers nearby.

Paul opened the paper wrapping and bit into the burger. He realized he didn't have an appetite. He placed the burger back into the bag. He placed his face in his hands and resumed praying.

Lieutenant Inwood stood with two men in dark suits. Paul assumed the FBI. A lady walked towards them with a rolled copy of the building plans for Mt. Sherman; it included the one and a half acreages on which the building set.

A breakthrough had come when Debra Martin, a family member, received a text message from her sister Linda's phone:

*"3 mn @ 1 wm."*

When Debra received this message around 12:00 p.m., she did not understand it. She'd tried to call Linda to see what it meant but Linda did not answer the phone. She probably set her rings to "silent" during services, Debra reasoned. It was after the news broadcast that she realized her sister was in trouble. Linda attended Mt. Sherman.

Debra called the police station as she headed to Mt. Sherman and gave the information she had received. When Debra made it to Mt. Sherman, the barricade had already started. She was able to explain the message. She was immediately allowed to go through. The message was clear.

"Three men and one woman. She is telling us how many gunmen there are." Debra was speaking to the Lieutenant.

Lieutenant Inwood became even more concerned. The original hope that there was only one gunman or maybe two was dashed. They had to contend with more obviously disturbed individuals. This increased the potential danger involved in securing the safety of the parishioners.

* * *

Jerod and Jonathan arrived almost at the same time. They stood outside. Yellow tape surrounded the proximity of the church. Jerod proceeded to go across the yellow. He lifted his leg.

"Sir, I'm going to have to ask you to not attempt to come across the line," an officer with a stern expression ordered Jerod.

Jerod hesitated then placed his leg back on the ground.

"Officer, my mom is in there," Jerod pleaded.

"That's understandable, but no one is allowed...."

"Please," Jonathan broke in. "We need to come officer."

The officer was unyielding.

"I've asked you to not cross this line. If you insist on it, I'm going to have to arrest you both for obstruction of justice."

44

Jerod and Jonathan relented to the fact that they had no other choice but to wait with the others. All stood together. Some had more at stake than others. Some close to tears with fear. Some full of anticipation and curiosity.

One spectator looked up into the sky and saw the gathering of clouds. They seemed to fold in some uniform fashion as the skies seemed to roll over this area above Mt. Sherman. Perhaps it was going to rain. Out of nowhere, the wind suddenly seemed to be getting stronger as people stood. Some decided to get back into their cars. Neighbors and people who lived within walking distance decided rain was coming and they had better get to the shelter of their home. Many who had loved ones in Mt. Sherman took no heed to the rising wind or the potential rain. They stood waiting.

*...Stand and see the salvation of the Lord....* *(2Chronicles 20:17—KJV)*

\* \* \*

In the small room, some of the mothers were on their knees. Some lay prostrated as they were drenched in the presence of God. Singing, praying, and rejoicing. Oh, how long had they been praying and singing? There was no time to think about Sunday dinner. No time to consider the fall festival program, the senior citizen outing, the various activities of Mt. Sherman. Never had they spent so much time in prayer! Never had they experienced such joy! Strangely the thoughts of the gunmen were replaced by thoughts of the Father. Hearts and minds soley on the Father, His Son, and The Holy Ghost. No one wanted such a communion to end.

God's angels stood protectively around the mothers; their fervent prayers made as a result of their plight drew the attention of God and His angels.

*"Are they not ministering spirits for those who are the heirs of salvation?" (Hebrews 1:14—KJV )*

"Holy, Holy," the angels sang. The mothers too sang praises to the Father. Praises they had never sung before. Sure they had experienced joyous times in church as the choir sang. Various programs had elicited moving moments in church. But this? This was something so much deeper. More intimate, more real.

The songster smiled as she spoke with God with her heart.

God: "My daughter."

"My God, my Savior, my refuge," she replied.

God: "I have ordained you to praise me."

Her heart was elated. "Oh Lord, you are my God, earnestly I seek you. My soul thirst for you...."

The love between God and His people. The intimacy He longs for. The fullness of His presence. No barriers, only hearts for Him. God's eyes, always seeking to and fro to show Himself strong to those who love Him. (2 Chronicles 16:9—KJV)

With love and kindness He draws His people daily. Satan's tactics distracts and steal the glances owed to God.

The shame of this realization lays crouched in a dark corner now. There is not even any place for shame. No condemnation. Just now. Now moments with the Father, the Son, the Holy Ghost.

God smiles as a Father would as He looks upon His children basking in sincerity and truth, loving Him—simply loving Him.

\* \* \*

Fieldmnan gave the orders to the congregation. "Throw your bibles in the aisles, your word, your sword, you call it." Condescendingly.

They began slowly, one by one, to relinquish their bibles. Some expensive, some old and new. Brenda, without much thought, passed her bible to the aisles. The young lady and young gunman began clearing the bibles. They bagged them in large trash bags, carrying them to the front of the church.

Fieldman looked over at the right side. Those who professed to be true Christians. He then surveyed the left, those who did not claim the title of "Christian." Of the 400 members present, he estimated over twenty-five percent denied ownership of Christianity. He watched as the bibles were cleared from the aisles as the gunmen gathered them from each row.

Interestingly enough, some of the members began to weep as they gave the gunmen the "sacred" book. It was not realized until this moment that this book held their trust as though it was the very one in whom they trusted.

Is it not written, in the beginning was the word and the word was God and the word was with God? The precious pages held the inspired words dictated by God Himself. What was he going to do with the bibles? At this moment, they felt stripped.

The Pastor immediately contemplated how often he had spoken of Psalms 119 in which the psalmist stated, "I have hidden your word in my heart...."

Joycelyn's eyes began to flood. Droplets of tears fell. As a child, she remembered reading one of the Psalms. The Twenty-Third Psalms. In her mind, for the first time in years, she tried to remember.

"The Lord is my Shepherd. The Lord is My Shepherd." She stopped again.

"He...." She struggled to recapture the familiarity of something lost so long ago.

"He lay. He makes me to...." She was not sure. She hadn't thought of this in so long.

She held on to the few words she could remember, "The Lord is My Shepherd." She repeated this in her mind over and over again. The tears seemed to fall in unison with her heart as it stretched, opening to receive this truth.

If one could search the thoughts, it would be noted that many of the members, at this moment, struggled to recall bible scriptures and verses. Many who had been attending Mt. Sherman for years could not recall the words of the Twenty-Third Psalms.

"The Lord is My Shepherd. I shall not want," began to trail the thoughts as though it was a chant. Seeking some type of power in a powerless situation.

The tears of many began to fall from the convictions in their hearts that they did not hide much of the word of God in their hearts. So many Sunday, Wednesday and Friday night services. When all they had to do was "turn to" a particular scripture as it was read or expounded upon.

Many who failed to open the books daily at home or on their jobs during break, or even while waiting at the doctor's office. The conviction that no real time was given to meditate on God's word day and night... instead of just on Sunday.

The Holy Spirit moved among those whose hearts held these conviction. He whispered the question.

"Do you have enough of me, the word, in your heart to sustain you? Can you recall my promises from the tablets of your heart? I have written on the hearts of those, that which they have meditated on. I will bring back unto your remembrance what I've taught you."

***Blesseth is the man...his delight is in the law of the Lord and in it does he meditate day and night.... (Psalms 1:1-2)***

Across the room both the left and right, members fell on their knees weeping, crying with regret.

* * *

The gunmen seemed fascinated yet suddenly on guard as they witnessed the literal weeping of the members as they seemed to have simply let go of any posture of any stance.

Fieldman muttered. "Babies, you'd think I'd taken their bottles."

Reginald chuckled at the chiding remark.

Mae stood with her gun. The nervousness she'd felt earlier in the room with the old women began to creep up her spine. It was with great effort that she kept her face passive in the view of this display of helplessness.

"Why don't we just take what we came here for and go?" she thought.

The young gunman, though with no emotional connection to the weeping of the people, found it disconcerting. "I am ready to get this over with." Unknown to him, his sentiments were the same as Mae's.

Mae began to retrace her steps in her mind; how is it that she was now holding a gun in church? She began to think about her tumultuous upbringing.

* * *

Mae had been orphaned at the age of four. Many years were spent in foster homes in the State of Nebraska. She was passed from one foster home to the next. Mae had never felt like she belonged anywhere. She was angry most of the time and acted out as a result of this. It affected her grades. Her behavior became too much for the foster parents, and she was always being reassigned to make the lives of others as hellish as her own. At the age of fourteen, she was

49

taken to Mimi Foster, a robust, black woman in her late fifties.

She remembered the day she met Mimi Foster. The social worker took her to the door, rang the doorbell and when the door opened, there she stood. No smile, just a look—stern, yet not mean.

"Here she is," the social worker's tone was indifferent. Translation:

"Here is this bad behind child who is hopelessly lost and we know we will probably have to reassign her to someone else in a couple of weeks, because she is not going to fit in here either. Just keep her until then and we will pick her up again and find some other stupid foster home to take her for a while."

Mae's small suitcase held a couple of pants and shirts and several changes of underwear. Her only shoes were on her feet.

Mimi shook her head to indicate "ok" and nodded to Mae to come in. Mae stepped inside. Mimi's voice was smooth and calm.

"Thank you, Mrs. Jefferson." No other comment.

The social worker, anxious to leave, turned and walked briskly down the steps to her car and sped off.

Mae stood quietly looking around. The first thing she noticed was the big black book on the coffee table. It was a bible.

Mimi Foster closed the door, turned and looked directly into Mae's eyes and said.

"You are here because God wants you here. If God wants you here, then we are happy to have you."

She called for her husband, Jack Foster and the other foster children, Bradley and Gina, and introductions were made. Bradley was fifteen. He'd been with Mimi since he was nine. Gina was sixteen. She had been with Mimi since she was two; they hugged Mae and told her welcome. She didn't understand why but for the first time she felt like she was finally home.

Mae learned quickly that her new foster parents were referred to as "Mama Mimi" and "Daddy Foster."

This black book on the table was read each morning by Mama Mimi or Daddy Foster. It was at this time she started attending church for the first time. Her previous foster parents didn't make the foster children attend church. Here, every Sunday morning and Wednesday night, she and her new family attended church.

Mama Mimi loved to sing. She sang in the mornings and in the afternoons. When Mae came home from school, even at night, she'd hear Mama Mimi singing hymns they sang in church.

"Yes Jesus Loves Me" became Mae's favorite. She loved to hear Mama Mimi sing. Mae caught herself singing similar tunes as she did her chores around the house. She wanted to stay in this place. It was so peaceful here. More than anything, she was loved. After all, Mama Mimi had said, "We are happy you are here!"

For the next three years, she was transformed into a young lady with decent grades. She participated in activities held in their little multi-cultural church where she learned about God. Mama Mimi and Daddy Foster were highly respected. When people saw them it was, "The Fosters and their children." Ironically enough, they were never referred to as "foster" children. Bradley and Gina were like real brothers and sisters Mae never had.

* * *

It was the summer before her senior year in high school. Mae had just been hired at a local grocery store within walking distance of her home. Excitedly she was

51

rushing home to tell Mama Mimi the good news. Bradley and Gina had already graduated from high school; Bradley had joined the Navy, and Gina attended college several states away. She called and visited as often as she could.

Mae turned the corner and in front of her home was an ambulance. She ran just as the paramedics were rolling the cot out of the house. Mama Mimi! Her eyes were closed. The paramedics quickly explained she had suffered a stroke. Daddy Foster was crying. He wanted Mae to stay near the telephone. He would be in contact. He got in the back of the ambulance, the paramedics closed the door and Mama Mimi was quickly driven to the hospital.

Mama Mimi was in Intensive Care for two weeks. She drifted into a coma. Apparently this was too hard for Daddy Foster. A month later, Daddy Foster died from a massive heart attack. Bradley and Gina came home for the funeral. Mama Mimi had to be sent to a nursing home facility for twenty-four hour care.

The state officials sought to reassign Mae. Mae's heart was broken. Bradley lived on a ship. She couldn't live with him. Gina's lodging was on the campus of the school she attended. That was out of the question.

The neighbors, Mr. and Mrs. Brinkman, were members of the same church as the Fosters. They persuaded the officials to allow Mae to stay with them temporarily so as not to upset the progress she'd made over the years with the Fosters.

Mae was grateful. She had often run errands for Mrs. Brinkman when Mama Mimi sent her to the store. She basically just spoke to Mr. Brinkman. She rarely saw him, except at church.

Mae did not start the new summer job after Mama Mimi's stroke. A few weeks before school started, she was awakened during the night by a looming figure. Her scream was cut off by a large hand that covered her mouth.

Mr. Brinkman whispered, "Shush. Don't say anything. It's ok."

Mae lay rigid unsure of what to do. He began to grope at the buttons on her top searching for entrance. She squeezed her eyes closed telling herself she was dreaming. She stiffened with repulsion as she felt his hands on her bare flesh. He told her that this was the least she could do to show how grateful she was for him and his wife's generous offer, allowing her to stay under their roof and all. She didn't fight him as he pulled down her panties.

Mae was in shock. After Mama Mimi, Daddy Foster, then this! She became numb. Mr. Brinkman was one of the leaders in their church. He told her that no one would believe her if she told. He also reminded her that she had nowhere else to go. For some reason, Mae believed this. For the next few months through high school, Mae silently endured the abuse once and sometimes twice a week.

Mrs. Brinkman was oblivious to the decadence that was taking place in her home, by her husband. Mrs. Brinkman was very kind to Mae. She saw to it that Mae had adequate clothing and school supplies. Yes, she even took her to visit Mama Mimi in the nursing home every other weekend. For a time, these visits served as Mae's lifeline. It was here that Mae could hope.

Mae would sit with her and sing the songs Mama Mimi had sung. She prayed that her Mama Mimi would wake up and rescue her again. Then Mae would feel the peace she'd become so accustom to. Mama Mimi never woke up.

The Brinkmans didn't read the Bible at home. They didn't even demand that Mae attend church. Mae had begun to look at church as an illusion. All sense of what she had received from Mama Mimi and Daddy Foster slowly ebbed away along with the hope that one day Mama Mimi would wake up.

Though barely, she managed to keep passing grades. She remembered how important her graduating was to Mama Mimi. On the same day of graduation, she took her diploma to the rehabilitation center to show Mama Mimi. Tears rolled down Mae's face as she placed the diploma under Mama Mimi's lifeless hands. She knew that she could no longer bear to return to this place. She brushed the tears away as she opened the door and closed it behind her. She didn't even whisper goodbye, and she didn't look back.

The next day, Mae hitchhiked until she arrived in Newark, New Jersey. Believing she could possibly start a new life, she found a job at a local gas station. Eventually she met and got involved with a wild crowd where she learned about marijuana and drinking heavily. It numbed the pain that tore at her heart each day.

A few months later she took a job as a dancer at one of the clubs to make more money. She tried calling the rehab a few times to check on Mama Mimi, but she finally gave up after countless responses of "We are sorry, there is still no change in her condition." Mama Mimi never woke up.

So many years had passed and so quickly. It had been nearly ten years since she'd left Nebraska. She met Reginald and it seemed to be they should be together. She stood suddenly startled by an abrupt order.

"Mae, over here."

She came back to the present. The congregation looked depleted in their conviction.

She noticed the old lady who'd said earlier, "Young lady, we can't all walk." She was staring at Mae. Mae quickly turned to the attention of Fieldman.

* * *

Bernard lay still in the choir room. Suddenly he heard a voice. He woke up.

God: "My son. Gird up."

Bernard sat up. He looked around the room. No one. He placed his hands on the wound in his side. The bleeding had stopped. He placed both feet on the floor. He seemed to have been rejuvenated somehow. He stood up. He took the towel from his side. He used the gauze from the medicine kit and wrapped his waist. He heard voices; they were closer. He quickly replaced the towel and lay back down on the sofa. Motionless.

Reginald's voice. Bernard heard the door open. The young gunman was with him.

"Man, what is Fieldman doing? Man I thought you said we were robbing these hypocrites then leaving."

Reginald's voice whispered, "Look we will be getting out of here soon!"

Cedric was troubled. "Man, the police are out there. How are we going to get out of here? Damn, man. How?"

Reginald scoffed. "Man, just shut the hell up, will ya?"

"Fieldman, he's...," Cedric hesitated. "he is crazy, man." Cedric looked over at Bernard's body. "And I've killed a man!" Cedric suddenly seemed petrified. "Man. Hey, Man!" He started walking towards Bernard.

"Shut up, Cedric!" Reginald commanded. "Look over in the closet and see if there is any rope or something we can use to tie with."

Cedric hesitated then turned away from Bernard and proceeded towards the closet. Reginald started back out the door.

"Bring what you find."

Cedric shook his head. Unsure of why he was doing what he was doing. The door closed.

* * *

Cedric was a high school dropout. He lived with his aging grandmother and worked for below minimum wages at one of the local mechanic shops. He was a regular at the bar where Mae danced. Cedric met Mae a few years earlier when he had to fix the brakes on an old beat up Volkswagen Mae was driving. Mae had invited him to the bar where she worked. Cedric went. He was quite fascinated by Mae, but their relationship was strictly friends. Cedric never pursued more. He was happy to just have Mae as a friend. Cedric didn't have many friends and was somewhat of a misfit. He wasn't very sociable.

Cedric noticed Reginald a few times; most of the time Reginald was alone. One night he struck up a conversation with Reginald. They seemed to acknowledge each other afterwards. One night after Mae had finished dancing, Cedric had promised to give her a lift home. When she came over to where Cedric and Reginald were sitting, Cedric introduced them. Reginald and Mae hit it off immediately. It wasn't long after this that they became a couple. They were inseparable.

Reginald had told how Fieldman and he had met at one of the crazy hospitals. Actually it was some place where they both were receiving counseling. Counseling was part of Reginald's parole requirements. Fieldman's doctor had referred Fieldman because he felt Fieldman needed help in coping with his wife's death. Somehow during group counseling they found that they shared something. They both had a loathing for "Christians." Fieldman invited Reginald over for coffee. Reginald became Fieldman's friend.

They often discussed the various Christian programs which seemed to have inundated television. They were obsessed with ridiculing the miracles and healing services of evangelists. When the plan to prove that the Christians were hypocrites was conceived, neither could say. Reginald's talk was more the talk of his wretchedness. Fieldman, on the other hand, had more sinister plans.

Fieldman had become enthralled with various organizations such as the Atheist Alliance and The Atheist United. His interest in Christian News was reports of the persecution of the Christians in various countries. He felt that the Christians got what they deserved.

Fieldman applauded an Anti-Apostasy movement (AGAP) led by a man name Muhammad Mu'min Al-Mubarak, a Muslim radical who is a former Christian who had converted to Islam. Mu'min had a passion to eradicate Indonesia of Christianity, which was rapidly growing throughout the country. In essence, Mu'min was a Paul who became a Saul.*

Reginald enjoyed Fieldman's knowledge of facts and information of the Bible. Fieldman took glee in reports of anti-Christian gains around the world. He kept Reginald informed of churches forced to close in various countries. AGAP was becoming highly effective in pressuring the local governments to close churches.

In many European countries, he knew that Christianity showed a decline, and it was being predicted that Islam would become the continent's dominant faith.

Of course, the Islam religion was of no interest to Fieldman, but its infiltration of Christianity served to feed a part of his desire. He wanted to prove the flaws of Christianity.

Now, Reginald was a bit uncertain of Fieldman's plans at this point. Although he did not voice it to Cedric, he knew Fieldman's pain of losing his wife, Dorothy. Fieldman would talk about sacrifices given for people, all due to his love for her. It wasn't until her death that he decided to deal with the truth. He didn't truly know this God his wife seemed to know so well. Fieldman and Dorothy shared their lives. When she died, it was like Fieldman had nothing left to share.

Reginald realized his money was running out. He couldn't find a job. His life was in shambles. When Fieldman told him about his plans to rob the offering plate of the hypocrites—church folk—he said count him in. Robbing from a bunch of hypocrites didn't seem to be the worst of ideas. He'd been robbed emotionally by several of these so-called "Christian" brothers and sisters—his wife and her lover.

Reginald had left Cedric in the choir room. He needed to check back in the adjacent sanctuary.

* * *

The members were quiet. Waiting. Reginald eyed the non-Christians. Brenda sat nervously as he swept his focus her way. Mrs. Evans, by this time had convinced herself that she wouldn't be killed and that was good enough. Yet she couldn't help the empty feeling inside her being. So void....

One of the babies started crying. Reginald turned towards the mother. The mom was in the process of getting a bottle out of the diaper bag. The bag fell over and the bottle with a couple of other items rolled out. Reginald reached down and picked up the bottle. He reached out to give the bottle to the mother. The woman's hands were shaking as she took the bottle from his hands. She did not look up. At this time Reginald surveyed the room looking at the children present. They really served no point in this. He walked over to Fieldman and whispered hesitantly, "What about these kids?"

"What about 'em?" Fieldman's voice held no concern.

"Why don't we let them go?" Reginald paused. "They really serve no purpose."

Amazingly, Fieldman shrugged his shoulder. "Get them out, let them go then. That's your call."

Reginald couldn't explain why he made such a suggestion, much less why Fieldman agreed with him.

Fieldman called Mae over.

In a low tone he said, "Get me a head count of children and toddlers."

Mae started counting the toddlers who were sitting with their mothers. In total, toddlers with the infants, there were twelve. Except for an occasional cry, the children were amazingly pretty quiet. Mothers managed to lay three and four year olds on the bench and they slept peacefully, unaware of what was taking place. When all the other children were added, Mae counted a total of twenty-five (infants, toddlers, and children up to age eighteen).

* * *

Outside the wind blew around Mt. Sherman. Several television stations waited patiently for any sign of action, wanting to be the first to report. Inside many Christian mothers were praying fervently for the safety of their children.

The angels stood waiting for any cue, any order from the Holy One. Before time as we know it, they have stood ready day and night—sometimes to protect, sometimes to open doors, sometimes even to close them. With anticipation and gladness, they readily face the "fallen angels" everyday. God charges them to guard the humans who served him "in all their ways. So that their feet do not dash upon a stone." (Psalms 91)

The battles were increasingly fierce as time passed. Satan's tactics are desperate because even in the heavenlies, the celestial beings sense that the Great One will soon end Satan's rulership on the earth.

Satan, the deceiver, the liar of lies. Time long ago when the lead praiser of angels was cast out of the heavens with his followers, these angels witnessed it. They witnessed the top praiser's arrogance even after he lost his position in heaven. They were indignant that such rebellion would take place in heaven. They were fierce in their loyalty to the Great I Am.

I Am commanded each for certain duties. The joy of being in his employ was compounded with being his creation. How wonderful! They watch man's daily practices. Man's choice to serve the one and true God was met with great celebrations in the heavens. The angel that carried Fieldman's wife from earth rejoiced with the other angelic beings as they all knew the Father's joy for:

*"How precious in the sight of God is the death of his saints." (Psalms 116:15--KJV)*

This same angel was among the many who rejoiced with the Father at Dorothy's "new birth." She gave her life to Jesus at an early age. The age of nine to be exact.

* * *

Years ago, strangely enough, Mother Mary Johnson and Fieldman's wife, Dorothy, had been best friends since grade school. That was, they were best friends until their Freshman year in college. This is when Dorothy met Fieldman. When she brought Fieldman to meet Mary, she could tell that he was captivated by Dorothy. Mary found out that in order to gain Dorothy's affection, he did whatever he had to in order to keep it. Even if it meant perpetrating a love for her God.

One day Dorothy came back to the dormitory to tell Mary about her engagement to Fieldman. She told Mary that she and Fieldman planned to change their majors to religious studies and hoped to go into the mission fields. Mary knew that Fieldman's heart had no connection with a true relationship with God. Somehow Fieldman managed to take Dorothy's mind to the point of no return. Soon after graduation from college, Mary lost contact with Dorothy. Later Mrs. Johnson would remember Fieldman's identity and learn of Dorothy's death from breast cancer.

Mother Johnson was right. Fieldman didn't have a relationship with God. For many years, Fieldman was given the opportunities to know God, but Fieldman's heart held two masters. Dorothy sanctified her husband. Fieldman was a good husband; to many, a good man. Fieldman had never accepted God's Son as his personal Savior. No permission was given by God to heal Dorothy. The Father wanted her to come home.

The Holy One had sent the healing angel to Bernard after his prayer for strength. Bernard felt a great peace which was actually the presence of the Holy Spirit. Bernard went into a deep sleep. The angels circled Bernard as the Holy Spirit hovered over Brother Bernard. The healing presence had already started the healing process.

The God of all gods sent angels to do the bidding of the young mothers' prayer request that their children be safe. The legion of angels were of such that the "fallen ones" had to retreat… for a while.

* * *

"Ok, I have news for you." Fieldman's voice was startling. As time passed, no one understood his plans.

"Yes, I have news." The congregation looked at Fieldman. His voice was so unreadable.

"I'm allowing children to be excused. Infants are to be given to the teenagers." Several teenagers grabbed the hands of parents, family members, friends; they trembled. They had witnessed the brutality of these gunmen. Mr. Bernard was dead. The thoughts of what would become of them reflected on the faces of the adults as well as the children.

"You pathetic imbeciles. Do you wish your children to die with you?" Fieldman seemed to sneer.

His face seemed to be even more hideous as time passed along with patience. Fieldman was slowly losing his mind. That was becoming clearer by the moment. Members looked at each other for answers. Unspoken but clear. Perhaps this is God's mercy for the children. Perhaps....

Friedman went ballistic. "Get your stupid asses this way. Now! I have no tolerance for your leisure!"

Parents pried loose the hands of their children as they coaxed them to let go. Mae stood waving the gun directing the children to one of the corridors of the church. Mothers praying for their children knew that this was God's call. Joycelyn hugged her three babies. She looked and made eye contact with her eight year old, nodding towards the babies. The eight-year old, with tears streaming down her cheeks, understood as she and the other children were hurriedly ushered out by the three gunmen.

The scratching sound of the old door opening on the side entrance of the church took the outside audience by surprise. The local media was waiting.

"Look!" Staggard quickly directed the cameraman. "Get this quickly." The man on cue, got in position, focusing the lens as he, along with several other cameramen, took advantage of this new event in "today's news."

Lieutenant Inwood gave orders, "Don't shoot! Hold tight!" Orders given through the radio he held. The policemen were armed and ready.

Paul's eyes widened as he saw the sixteen-year old, Stephanie Green, holding an infant. Several older children he recognized were carrying babies and baby bags. Several toddlers walked with older children as they held their hands, leading them to safety.

"We are not sure, but it looks like some of the hostages are being released. Well, actually children, toddlers, and infants are being released. There are no signs of adults," Staggard spoke as she noted the release from the church's side entrance.

Waiting family started crying out names towards the children. Children looked to see aunts, uncles, cousins, grandmas, familiar faces.

Cathy Staggard, an expert in this arena and knowing how to seek out an opportunity, motioned the cameraman to a sobbing twelve year old, as the policemen sought to keep control of family and friends who threatened to break through the barricade. "My Nana...my Nana!" The girl, with two ponytails, stood alone crying, heart-wrenching tears flowed in between her struggle to talk.

Obviously traumatized and shaken by the pass events. Hopelessly, she simply crouched onto the pavement; she sat with her hands brushing away an endless flow of tears, her body heaving from the emotions inside. One of the officers walked over and lifted the little girl up in his arms. She wrapped her arms around his neck crying pitifully. "Everything is going to be all right. You are safe now! Shush! It will be ok, I promise...."

No one seemed to notice the rolling clouds over Mt. Sherman. As God's voice rumbled through the clouds, those present heard thunder.

*I cried to my God for help. From his temple he heard my voice. My cry came before him unto his ears... He parted the heavens and came down... The Lord thundered from heaven. The voice of the most high resounded. (Psalm 18:6-13—KJV)*

No one seemed to notice that the wind was only blowing around Mt. Sherman. Nearby homes received a portion of the wind as it blew but had they looked closer, they would have seen the concentrated area in which the wind and rolling clouds revolved.

Police officers gathered the children together. Several vans quickly arrived. The children were placed in the vans and driven to the nearby hospital, and then to be reunited with the closest relatives.

As the children were being gathered, Cathy Staggard had swiftly taken the cameraman to a closer angle towards the door in which the children exited. As she held her microphone to her mouth, the cameraman started focusing to get a clear shot. His eyes gazed suddenly to her left. He started frowning, blinking, and wiping at his eyes trying to clear his vision. He could have sworn that he was looking at the lower half of an enormous and very tall man in a white robe; it looked like some type of sash was hanging down from the middle. Just as suddenly, one of the officers tapped him on the shoulder with orders for him and Cathy Staggard to step backwards. They were too close to the proximity that was to be controlled. They obeyed the order.

Cathy was puzzled by the cameraman's expression. She was about to ask him what, but he was shaking his head. He raised his hands to indicate he didn't want to speak at that moment. Staggard thought he was, like many, affected by the emotions expressed by the children. This, she concluded, was something most distressing to say the least. She didn't ask any questions. She ended her report with,

"This was a pivotal moment for many as we continue to watch with hope that more hostages will be released. The authorities have been able to identify one of the four gunmen. One who is seemingly the leader, James Fieldman, is a former student and missionary of the Presbyterian Theological Seminary. A bit of irony to this unexplainable atrocity against the members of one of the oldest, most respected churches in Newark, New Jersey. We will update you as we learn more about the other gunmen. Cathy Staggard reporting live."

Camera off. The glistening eyes of the cameraman did not go unnoticed.

Cathy, softly, "William. What is going on?"

William had been with Cathy for years. He was not just a cameraman. He was a confidant as well.

"Cathy, have I ever lied to you?"

Cathy smiled smugly, playfully hitting him on the shoulder.

"No, you dummy. You know you don't have that much nerve. I'd knock you out with your own camera."

William, still looking. No smile.

Cathy was deeply concerned. Something had made William very uncomfortable.

"What is it, William?"

Cathy placed a hand on his arm.

"What happened, William?" Trepidation was slowly creeping up her back, her neck.

He placed the camera on the bed of the news truck. He turned to Cathy and almost straining he said, "I... saw... an angel by the side entrance door. Don't ask me how I know this, but as I noticed this, something seemed to be telling me that he was there to protect. My God, Cathy, an angel!"

William broke down weeping. Cathy placed her hand on his shoulder as comfort, as she realized this was...Cathy had no words. She simply pondered on what her friend had just said to her.

* * *

Bernard was careful as he silently rose from the sofa. Cedric was in the closet pulling out boxes that held donated clothes and other items such as shoes, socks, etc. He was regretting coming with the others. He was way over his head.

Cedric didn't know what hit him as Bernard swiftly grabbed Cedric's neck. Cedric didn't have a chance to make a sound. Bernard pressured the crucial points on his neck and shoulders. Cedric struggled for a few seconds, floundering; slowly he relinquished his strength. Bernard's sleepy hold. He hadn't done that in years! It would have been a simple thing to just break Cedric's neck, but Bernard felt God preferred he just subdue him, for now.

Bernard picked Cedric up. Throwing him over his back, he walked carefully to the door. He opened it slightly to listen. Bernard did not notice the paper along with the thin, worn wallet that fell out of Cedric's pockets. He heard Fieldman and the other gunmen as they ushered the children out the side entrance opposite of the choir room.

As massive as he was, he displayed agility as he carefully carried Cedric down the hall to one of the closet doors. Unknown to most, this was really a door that led to the cellar. Washers, dryers, vacuums, and cleaner materials were kept here; there were also old costumes and materials and supplies for decorations.

Bernard grabbed several ropes from one of the boxes and tied Cedric's hands and ankles together. He also tied a muffler across his mouth. What he did not need was for Cedric to regain consciousness and make problems. He hurried back upstairs just in time to hear Fieldman's order, "Now, close it and lock it."

Bernard eased back into the choir room. He pushed in clothes and boxes where Cedric was searching for ropes. He closed the closet doors. He quickly replaced the towel and lay back down on the sofa, willing his body to be rigid.

"Father," Bernard prayed, "I know you're with me. Please, Father, show me how to rescue my dad and the others. Father, let them come to no harm."

*And God's ears are not so far he cannot hear nor is his arms too short he cannot save. (Isaiah 59:1—KJV)*

God revealed to Bernard that the angels were dispatched to assist in the safety of the children. At every corner of the sanctuary, there was an angel, strong, mighty, and ready to minister to the heirs of salvation. *(Hebrews 1:14)*

\* \* \*

Lieutenant Inwood was encouraged by the release of the children; however, the information they provided was disconcerting. During questioning, the children told of Fieldman's commands that "true" Christians move to one side of the church and the plans were to "kill all the Christians." They also told about the shooting of Brother Bernard and their observation that he was, indeed, dead.

The church's construction plans revealed an attic window that may give access to the sanctuary. The children were also able to tell that the elderly mothers were escorted to another room. No gunfire was heard, so they could only assume that they had, as yet, not been harmed.

\* \* \*

Fieldman looked around for Cedric. "Where is he?"

"Who?" Reginald asked.

"That damn Cedric. The fool. I haven't seen him in a while."

Reginald stated, "Well, he is looking for some ropes in the room down the hall." Reginald pointed in the direction of the choir room.

"That minuscule brained, miserable nitwit. Where is he?"

Reginald thoughts were traveling with pure aggravation.

"Let me go see what's keeping him." Reginald started towards the hall.

"No," Fieldman ordered, "Let me."

It was evident that the threat in his voice was just a precursor to his imminent demise of Cedric.

Fieldman had only agreed to include Cedric at Reginald's persistence that more manpower would ensure a quicker, more effective implementation of the planned robbery. Of course, now it was clear that robbery was far from Fieldman's mind.

Reginald touched Fieldman's arm to insist he let him go. Fieldman shrugged Reginald's hand.

"Keep your eyes on this pietistic group of...." Fieldman did not finish. He hurried, with purpose, towards the choir room.

When Fieldman reached the choir room, he hesitated. It took effort to restrain the rage that was threatening by the minute to burst forth. He turned the knob. As he entered, he saw the body of the man who was shot earlier. He lay on the sofa.

"Rigor mortis has probably set in by now," Fieldman thought. No remorse.

Fieldman continued inside the room. "Cedric!" he muttered under his breath. He noticed the closet. He opened it. Nothing. Only robes and boxes of clothes. He looked around the room. The stain-glassed window showed twilight. The shadows of tree limbs moved with the blowing wind outside.

*"...He makes his angels winds." (Hebrew 1:7-NLT)*

"Where are you, Cedric?" He glanced back at the man on the sofa.

"Did his abdomen move?"

He was about to look closer, and as his foot came down he heard the crackling of paper. He had stepped on something. Paper. Next to it was a wallet. Curious, he bent down and picked up the paper and wallet. He looked inside the wallet. It was Cedric's. Stupid idiot.

As he held the paper, he got a strange feeling down his spine. He began to unfold the paper, carefully. The room seemed to be spinning as he read the words.

"I came to visit you today. I received your letter. I am here at 1143 Wellmington Street, the address on the return address of your envelope. I will try again. If you visit, please introduce yourself to me. God bless. Signed. Pastor, Mt. Sherman Community Church."

Fieldman did not understand this. His mind flashed back when they were hurrying to the van. He remembered wondering what Cedric was doing. He saw him picking up the paper. He needed to hurry. Fieldman had seen this paper, but had not bothered to pick it up, now that he thought about it.

He did not understand. However, he was going to get to the bottom of this. He searched the church. He came to the room where the old women were. He heard the singing, the praying. He stopped at the door. Instinctively, he backed away. His mind quickly returned to Cedric. "Where is he?"

"Bam!" he heard a gun shot. He began running back towards the sanctuary.

* * *

Some of the parishioners had managed to cause a diversion and was closing in on Reginald. Reginald had fired a warning shot. Fieldman looked over at the Pastor maliciously. Why did he hate him so much?

The congregation on both sides were huddled together, squatting behind the pews for the most part. Ten of the men were circling Reginald. Fieldman cocked the .357 in his hands.

"Yes!" he sneered, "Let me get rid of more of you." One of the older men nudged another near him. They backed away from Reginald.

Fieldman was livid. "I say we start shooting!"

Reginald's adrenaline was high from the parishioners' sudden plan of attack.

"Fine with me!" Reginald agreed.

Fieldman fired a shot.

Ugh! Oh, God! One of the men fell down on the floor holding his left thigh. The blood began to seep then flow through his trousers. The men next to him began to pull him towards a pew.

Fieldman's eyes were glassy. He looked around at the others. "Next time, it will be higher!"

Several of the men helped the injured man to lie back on the pew. They took off their suit jackets to use against the flowing blood.

"Oh, my God! Oh!" the man groaned in agony.

"Please!" The Pastor was standing looking at Fieldman pleadingly. As a Shepherd, his heart was heavily concerned for the safety of the members. He did not think about his own safety.

Outside, upon hearing the shots, Inwood's patience was waning. The crowd had become increasingly restless. Many began screaming at the officers.

"What are y'all waiting on? Why aren't you in there? What the hell do you think you all are doing? People are getting killed."

The police force stood its ground, keeping the crowd at bay. Some family members attempted to call cell phone numbers of some of the parishioners.

The men on the roof had located the attic entrance. There was another level of wood that obstructed the entrance to the room.

Through radio contact, Inwood inquired. "Anything yet?"

The officer in charge relayed, "Yes, we are removing the obstruction. As soon as this occurs, we will be able to be lowered down into the corridor leading to the sanctuary. The problem is that we can't do this hurriedly without being heard."

Inwood ordered, "Do what you have to do, but in 30 minutes, be ready to get in through the passage way."

"Yes, Sir!" the officer responded. They used the silent screwdriver as they removed each of the wood obstruction.

Deborah Martin's phone rang. Deborah quickly hit the "talk" button.

"Linda! Oh, my God! Are you ok?"

She heard the faint voice of her sister as Linda whispered, "Yes, for now. Please tell them to help us." Deborah was near Lt. Inwood and now motioned to him. Linda was taking a chance. The gunmen were up at the front of the church. She was sure they could not see her as she kneeled on the floor behind one of the pews in the sanctuary.

Deborah asked, "What is going on?" She heard groaning in the background.

"The crazy man just shot one of the deacons in the leg. I'm so afraid," Linda's voice trembled.

Deborah held back tears as she told her, "Hold on, Sister. Hold on; they are coming…. "

The phone disconnected. Linda had seen the redhead woman moving back towards the aisles. She quickly hung up the cell phone thrusting it back in the pocket of her skirt.

Linda held her hands as though she was praying. Mae noted the woman, but she continued to walk down the aisle.

\* \* \*

Fieldman held the gun; he looked around wildly. His eyes seemed to be glazed over. His eyes glared cruelly. He walked over and grabbed the Pastor by the neck. He placed the gun in his back.

"Would you die for these people?"

His voice was testing.

"Would you?" He demanded an answer.

The Pastor silently prayed, "Father, your will be done."

"Let these people go, and let me die instead." His statement was clear and sure.

As Fieldman squeezed the back of the Pastor's neck, he prodded the gun in his side. The pressure of the barrel pressed painfully at the Pastor's rib-cage. The Pastor did not flinch. Suddenly, Fieldman released his neck. The gun still pressing. Fieldman used his hand to retrieve the note he'd found in the choir room from his pant pockets. He handed the note to the Pastor.

"Did you write this?" Fieldman's voice was cold and raspy.

The Pastor took the note. He opened it. "I'm here at 1142…." His handwriting was clear.

"Yes." As he answered, the Pastor realized this man was the very one who'd warned him that he'd be visiting.

The Pastor looked into the dark cool eyes of one who was very close to madness. The spirit that now resided inside was no doubt in full control.

"Damn you!" Fieldman's voice was rough. He took the butt of the gun and hit the Pastor squarely across his jaw.

The congregation stared helplessly as the Pastor fell on the floor, hands cupping his broken jawbone. The blood seeped across his face, his nose. He prayed.

"Father, your will. Please let your people be safe."

Reginald now stood with the automatic rifle warningly. Mae stood on the left side of the church. They both wondered about Cedric. They both wondered about themselves. They were at a point of no return.

* * *

Cathy Swaggard was still trying to handle what William had told her. She knew that today wasn't just a typical day of hostages and gunmen. Something unexplainable was taking place.

"Cathy!"

She turned. One of the junior editors was now on the scene. Jason Branson.

"Oh, hi, Jason. So you couldn't stay away from the excitement?"

She tried at a little sarcasm to cover up how shaken she really was. Not from the fact that lives were in danger as a result of the hostage situation at Mt. Sherman, but because she knew that William truly had seen an angel or something clearly not of this world.

Jason held out a large gold envelope. He wore a sacred grin like the cat that swallowed the canary.

"What?" She wore a questioning expression.

She took the envelope.

"What is this?" she asked as she began unfastening the metal prongs.

"You'll see!" He waited to see the expression on her face. Cathy began to smile as she realized what was in the envelope.

"Are these what I think they are?"

"Yes, ma'am!" He playfully swerved around and did a quick bow, pretending to remove a hat off his head, placing one hand behind his back in a grandiose fashion.

"Those, my dear, are the head shots of all four gunmen—of course, one of them is a woman.

"How?" Cathy's voice was incredulous as she stood staring at the treasure in her hands. Pictures and a disk with stored copies of the pictures and information.

Jason laughed heartily. Then mysteriously.

"My connections at the police department."

A surveillance camera on a nearby building caught the four as they walked towards the church's front steps leading to the entrance. Inwood had already compiled the information regarding the number and genders of the gunmen from the text message from one of the parishioners and the children's statements; the photos of the gunmen were revealed by the Department of Public Safety.

Cathy read the information underneath each of the photographs: James Fieldman, white male, height 6'4, blue eyes, blonde hair; Cedric also white male, height 5'4, brown eyes, auburn hair; Mae Jimerson, white female, height 5'3, brown eyes, red hair. Reginald Garrett was an African American male, 5'7, black eyes and hair. These faces. All enigmatic in that they aren't the faces of criminals. Cathy wondered what happened to make them hold an innocent congregation of people hostage?

Wearing a smile, Jason thrust his hands in his pant pockets as he observed Cathy. He was satisfied with the effect this had on Cathy. She was renowned for her acquisition of stories before many other reporters. Besides,

Jason had a special place in his heart for Cathy; of course, she had no idea. He planned to keep it that way.

As he started walking away, he said, "If you get it out now, you will beat the 6:00 news. Channel 43 will get first recognition.... "

He needn't continue. Cathy was already in the truck placing the enclosed disk in the computer to begin download.

William had regained some of his composure. He helped Cathy with the download and within twenty minutes they were ready to report.

Cathy stood. A professional, an impressive figure, confident, widely respected.

"We have just received vital information regarding the gunmen." The four pictures showed clearly on the screen.

"Reginald Garrett was released from prison a year ago after serving one year of a seven-year sentence on attempt of murder charges. The other three gunmen have no prior arrests or convictions. We've also received information that Mae Jimerson, Garrett's live-in lover, is a stripper at one of the local bars. Cedric Mitchell is described as a quiet loner who works as a mechanic at Boykin's Garage. James Fieldman, as previously reported, is a retired Presbyterian missionary and theologian."

Lisa Garrett stood almost numb. There on the 42-inch television screen was Reginald's mug shot along with pictures of the other gunmen who were holding members of Mt. Sherman hostage. Something seemed to catch in her throat. This was not the Reginald she'd married some years ago.

"Oh, my God!" The guilt crested through her soul as she reflected on the man he was before he found her and George in bed that night. Even now, she had no answers for her actions. Both she and George were married at the time.

Maybe the thrill of it all. Tasting that which was so forbidden. A taste that was still sour on her tongue.

"Hey, Lisa!" she heard George calling from the bedroom. She continued to stare at the screen, listening to the reporter's description of Reginald and the other gunmen.

"... an attempt of murderer, a stripper, a mechanic, and theologian makes a strange foursome for such a crime as we see here at Mt. Sherman. We will keep you posted as the local and federal authorities continue to unravel the motives and intents of these people. This is Cathy Staggard reporting live at Channel 43 News."

"No!" Lisa's voice screamed in her head. She is the reason for what he'd done. He just lost it that night.

After the arrest and even after he was sent to prison, she tried to contact Reginald. He wouldn't include her on the visitors list. She wrote him, but he never wrote back. He never spoke to her again after that night; she had crushed him.

George's wife divorced him. He had two teenage daughters who hated him. He was paying child support. Most of her money covered the house, the car. The worst part was she didn't even love George.

He called from the bedroom, "Baby, you coming?"

Unconsciously grimacing, Lisa rolled her eyes up in her head in frustration. She loathed sex with him. Yet, she was sorry for his disability. His left arm was useless. He also walked with a limp. Reginald's knife had damaged an artery and the loss of blood flow had caused irreparable damage. His job paid workman's compensation as he recovered from the assault. He had returned to his accounting job six months ago. Lisa felt that she deserved what she got. She wouldn't marry George that was for sure. They lived together, for now.

She brushed away the unwelcome teardrops that fell, preparing the way for a flood that she didn't want to explain to George. Sometimes she felt hatred for him. Her friends and family had no respect for her after what she'd done. Things were so different. She deserved this life she had. She had no joy. Nothing. Just living day after day with regrets.

She tried to go back to her church after this. She wanted so badly to cry out, "Help me!" She wanted to go before the church altar and beg for forgiveness from her church family; just as she had written to Reginald, asking him to forgive her. She asked God to forgive her, but in her heart she felt that she was too unworthy at this point. Why should He forgive her anyway?

The looks she received from some of the people, including her Pastor, Pastor Henderson, were of disgust. Some of the ladies acknowledged her with half smiles, but quickly found excuses to hurry on. Lisa still recalled some of the sermon that day.

"...thou shall not commit adultery!" Pastor Henderson's last look her way was in sync with "...fornicators and adulterous will go to hell!" Her heart was ridden with guilt. She craved solace. She knew her wrong.

Lisa turned the television off and walked slowly in the dark towards the bedroom. "It is interesting how you can adapt to darkness," she thought.

* * *

Bernard was crouched in the hallway waiting, knowing God would help him to help the people. Bernard saw the tall man as he drew back to hit Pastor. Suddenly, he knew that at this point the man was mad. If they were going to die, it wouldn't be without a fight.

As light as a cat and as massive as a full grown raging bull, he ran down the corridor and just as Reginald was turning to glance for who he thought would be Cedric,

Bernard leaped on Reginald with his fist swinging in full fury.

Wham! Bernard slammed a left hook under Reginald's chin. Reginald was falling from the first punch. The automatic rifle fell from his hands as Bernard swung another blow Right! Left! Right! Bernard knew that the might in which he was fighting was all from the strength of God. He did not hold back as he rendered every blow to Reginald's head, stomach, and face. The blood flew from Reginald's nose and mouth.

Fieldman had turned his attention from the Pastor just in time to see a swarm of members pouncing upon him. It was as though pent-up fear was unleashed in every swing and kick that landed on Fieldman's face and legs. His gun was wrenched out of his hand. Fieldman quickly tried to pick up the automatic rifle that Reginald had dropped.

Within seconds, one of the men grabbed Fieldman's wrist, twisting his arms behind his back. Fieldman yowled in pain as he felt his hand release the weapon. Several pushed Fieldman against the wall.

By now, Reginald was lying on the floor gasping for breath. Bernard stood over him sweating, heaving with sheer anticipation. In his mind, Bernard dared him to move, which would have given him another opportunity to loose some more blows. Parishioners were in shock seeing Brother Bernard, whom they thought was dead.

"Hold it!" Eyes turned towards the back of the church. Somehow Mae had managed to get the other automatic rifle that was hidden near the entrance and in the commotion was now standing, facing the crowd—aiming.

She saw Reginald. The blood! "Oh, my God! Oh Reginald." Reginald looked up, beaten with swollen eyelids.

Fieldman began to laugh, "Ha! ha! Yes! You fools!"

"Let them go! Or I will let every single round loose right now!" Mae's heart was pounding. She was so frighten, yet she knew she was in control.

The men loosened their grip on Fieldman's arms. Fieldman pushed their arms away angrily. "You B******s. Oh, you all will pay!"

Mae stood ready to pull the trigger.

"Yes, Jesus loves me! Yes, Jesus loves me! Yes, Jesus loves me.... "

The soft, serene voice of one of the old woman who couldn't walk. The congregation seemed mesmerized by the sudden sound of singing.

Mae turned her head in the direction of the singing. She looked, bewilderment on her face. It was then that she noticed the old woman's eyes, her face, even her nose. It was as though a veil was lifted from her eyes as she looked into the eyes of the old woman.

Mae's eyes began to fill with tears as she held the rifle. Still wielding it, yet her attention was on the old lady.

"Mama Mimi?" Her voice was a whisper.

The old lady stopped singing. "Yes, child," she said. So quiet, so calm.

"Mama Mimi!" Mae repeated. The room was so quiet yet Mae's voice was hardly heard. As this realization sank into the core of Mae's heart, her hand began to lower the rifle as she lowered the wall that had crept over her very being all these years.

Fieldman, realizing what was happening, suddenly reached over and before anyone could stop him grabbed Reginald's weapon from the floor and shouted, "Damn this!" He fired the automatic rounds into the crowd of parishioners.

He shot until there were no more bullets.

Bam! Bam! Circling the church as he pulled the trigger again and again. There was screaming. Members scurried for cover.

At this point the swat team felt no other recourse but to crash through the ceiling.

Inwood gave the orders to those outside.

"Go in now! Now!"

The police force burst through the doors, guns drawn. Ready. No ideas. Just pure urgency.

By the time the swat team had made it through the ceiling and down the hall to the sanctuary, Inwood and the other officers had crashed the church doors down. All ready.

The screaming, hollering, the cries had begun to subside.

At the front of the church, Fieldman was standing, holding an empty rifle. Every bullet was used. He was looking as though he had no idea where he was... disbelief on his face as he looked into the congregation around the room.

The Pastor was standing holding his jaw as he stood. He realized the pain from the butt of the gun was subsiding. The swelling and discomfort that was there a few minutes ago were not evident.

Fieldman stared blankly at the parishioners standing, including the man he'd shot in the leg earlier. Not to mention the man from the choir room sofa.

The old woman had her arms around Mae, holding and rocking her as Mae sobbed uncontrollably. She had found Mama Mimi.

Reginald was still on the floor in too much pain to move. He felt lost; the pain that assailed his head, his face, his stomach and his arms was unbearable. He knew his ribs were broken. He struggled with every breath.

Fieldman sat down on the front pew and just stared. He had no knowledge of who he was or where he was for that matter.

Inwood gave orders to handcuff Fieldman and Reginald.

Brother Benny was hugging his son Bernard. Both were crying, hugging each other, and praising God. Bernard told the officers where they could find Cedric.

Cedric was awake. He was helpless as they untied His binds. His rights were read.

The mothers were smiling and crying when they heard the turn of the lock in the door. Somehow, they knew it was time to leave this room. There was something new. Something now understood that wasn't understood before. Thoughts, no a mandate to come together to pray was on their minds. During this ordeal, God had given them his vision. They had time not only to speak to God, but to also listen—they heard from God.

How often they had shared in the traditional morning congregational prayers. Methodically. Many times it was repeated without true depth. Through the years it had been perpetuated. They operated on what most of them saw or was taught. Now, there will be a better course to show the younger.

Mama Mimi thanked God and cried as she held Mae. She had awakened three years and fifty pounds lighter from her coma after her stroke. She was shaken to find that not only had she had a stroke, which left her without the use of her legs, she'd also lost the love of her life—her precious Jack. The other two children were now married, and she saw them for holidays. But they had lost contact with Mae. She had no idea what had happened to Mae.

In order for her to be with family and to care for her, her sister, Eva, had brought her to Newark, New Jersey. Mae was told that the songster in the classroom was Mimi's older sister, Eva.

Fieldman and everyone present witnessed the firing of the gun. What could not be explained were walls and stained glass windows riddled with bullet holes; but none of the congregation members were injured or killed. How did the bullets miss the parishioners? Fieldman's mind went blank.

The Angels stood with great reverence as the Holy Spirit defrayed every bullet that sought to hit a parishioner. He allowed the bullets to penetrate the building and the windows. Under the total command of the Sovereign God, the Angels stood against the evil spirits whose desires are to steal, kill, and destroy.

Outside, hearing the shots, Jerod and Jonathan were thoroughly impatient and risking arrest both bolted pass the barricades as policemen started to smash in the doors to Mt. Sherman. Adrenaline was escalating as the people outside strained to find out more of what was going on.

The policemen stood next to Mae. Mama Mimi took out a handkerchief and wiped Mae's tears. Mae took the handkerchief, holding it to her face. She was spent from the release of tears that she had held inside for so many years. Yet, when she thought they were ending, more would flow.

"I love you, Mama Mimi."

"I know, baby. I love you too." Mama Foster's voice was soothing, calm.

Mae stood up. She stretched her arms out. She was handcuffed. She was led by one of the officers out of the sanctuary.

Jerod and Jonathan stood outside the door as each gunman and woman was led outside. The cameras flashed as local news reported the capture and arrest of the gunmen.

The crowd applauded as each was lead towards a police car that would take them to a home they would grow to loathe.

Fieldman simply looked around as though he was on a daily walk in the park. Just taking in the scenery. He looked from the left to the center to the right back to the center to left back again. Just looking with no expression.

Reginald's face was almost unrecognizable from the beating received from Bernard. His nose, his eyes. Everything swollen. Two officers stood on either side of the doors of an ambulance. They pulled open the doors for the paramedics. Reginald was helped in. The two officers went in behind Reginald along with one of the paramedics. The ambulance headed towards the nearest hospital.

Many of the members cried and thanked God. They began to hug each other. The members who disclaimed Christianity stood awkwardly as the unspoken knowledge illuminated the sanctuary. Nevertheless, no distinction was given as they hugged each other, thanking God for their safety.

The Pastor stood and walked up the two steps to the podium where hours before, he had been ordered down. By now many from the outside had joined in with the parishioners. The Pastor's jaw was not broken. Those who were near him saw the distortion, the swelling after Fieldman's hit.

Some of the congregation members tried still to reason, "Maybe he wasn't hit as hard as it seemed."

The man who was shot in the leg was now standing. The blood stained pants were the only proof left of his injury. He felt the area in his thigh. Where he was shot... no pain, nothing. He could not speak. His face told it all as the tears streamed down his face. He thanked the Father.

Pastor looked around the sanctuary. Jerod and Jonathon stood next to their mother. Arms locked around her. Mrs. Evans crying. Brenda saw Jerod. For a moment he saw her. Then just as quickly they both averted their eyes. Brenda knew that her life could never be as it was before. She knew she needed and wanted to know Jesus the Christ more than anything.

Craig stood rigidly; homosexuality was a way of life for him. To have it proclaimed in the opening brought a conviction of which he had no control. "Father," he prayed between tears, "help me."

"Let us pray." The Pastor bowed his head, as did those present.

"We hear you, Father. We understand what You allowed today. You have convicted our hearts and our minds. We are to be a light that will cause those who can't see to know that we are real and that through our lives, we will translate the 'realness' of Your Son to others. You have revealed to each of us our own hearts. Right now, we ask that through Your conviction that every heart present repent to You all their sins. Cleanse us and count us worthy of Your saving grace.

"Let each whom you have touched through this, draw closer to You. Our obedience is better than sacrifice. So we offer no sacrifice worthy, but our obedience to You—our one and true God. Thank You for today Father. Thank You for today for surely You have changed lives and with these changed lives, we will seek to change our communities, our city, our state. We will touch the world with what You have revealed to us today.

"As our slates have been washed clean, we began the walk that Your church should have, that we will no longer bring shame upon Your name as a result of hypocrisy and complacency. We will be without spot or blemish and those like the gunmen today will see Your truth in us. Forgive each of the gunmen who sought to harm your children. Father, help us to minister even unto them, that they will know Your son Jesus, in Jesus name. Amen!" The congregation agreed with "Amen."

Reverend Perkins walked with his head down, tears in his eyes. He could not wait to get home to call his ex-wife and tell her that he has forgiven her and to ask for forgiveness. Many had this posture as they had much to consider. Mrs. Evans walked down the steps of the church. She saw Joycelyn.

"Young lady!" Joycelyn turned to see who had called her.

Mrs. Evans walked a few steps to stand before Joycelyn. Mrs. Evans arms went around Joycelyn in a big sincere hug. Joycelyn sobbed against the woman who had earlier ignored her in church.

As Mrs. Evans released Joycelyn in order to wipe her own tears, she said, "Please give me a call sometime. If there is anything I can do to help you and your children, let me know."

Mrs. Evans looked in her purse and pulled out a pen. She tore a piece of notepaper from her wallet and wrote her phone number. She handed the paper to Joycelyn.

Joycelyn smiled. "Thank you."

Mrs. Evans felt such love towards her. She wanted to tell her then, but she controlled herself. She knew she would be able to show this young woman better than she could tell her at this time. Mrs. Evans smiled and walked back over to Jerod and Jonathan. Jerod insisted she ride with him. Jonathan drove behind them as they went to their mother's home.

"I'm going to start back going to church," Jonathan said out loud to himself. His heart felt different. He couldn't explain it, but he knew he had to get back in church.

Arrangements were made with the use of the church bus to pick up the children and safely return them to their parents. The Newark Police Department would assist in this.

* * *

Satan was angry about God's interventions. He nevertheless, planned to continue his mission to destroy as many Christians as he could before... even Satan feared his ending. He summoned his demons and they left the premises of Mt. Sherman. God had chosen this church to be an example for many. It was useless to stay in this place.

The rumbling of the clouds and the twilight became remnants as family members left Mt. Sherman. Greeting other family members and friends as God spoke:

"Awake my people. There is no time for complacency. Truly you will be persecuted for My sake. For you are a peculiar people. You are in this world, but not of this world. A people whose heart is towards Me. I will be your treasure. For My church is My bride. I will return. Be ready, for behold, I come quickly."

# CHARACTER ANALYSES

Pastor – Simply "Pastor." The "Utopia Pastor"--- His name will never be in the headlines for stealing, having an affair, using or selling drugs. He is one who fears and reveres God without hesitation. A deep love for the people God has entrusted him as Shepherd. This Pastor fits in God's mission. He desires to gather those who are lost.

Reverand Benjamin Perkins—People pleaser. Rarely preaches convicting messages. He weighs necessity of truth by his own scale of righteousness. Rather than confess or acknowledge his weaknesses, it is easier to skirt around it and pacify himself with the "Good News." The problem is he does not understand that the focal point of the "Good News" is "Sin." The "Good News" illuminates sin as a neon light, "Danger" which causes one to detour such a path and one will enter the arms of a Holy God.

The "Usher"—Smiling one. One who's seen as a Christian outwardly and totally happy in Jesus. Ready to serve at all times. Her life is worth more than her proclamation of Christ.

Mrs. Evans—One who operates in the "Nadab & Abihu spirit...." (Numbers 3:4) She does the things of God but does not seek the mind and heart of God. Also as the hypocrites in Matthew 6:1 who do the things of God to be given accolades, but her heart does not flow in her good deeds. She does charitable deeds before men to be recognized of men.

Brenda Benson—"Networking in Church." She is all about status and social gathering. Her weaknesses lay in the arms of a married man. Many times the word that she hears on Sunday is stolen by Satan's imps. The clattering sounds of her desires simply pushes the word of God aside—*My sheep hear my voice and follow me.* (John 10:27—KJV)

Jerod Evans—"Unfaithful husband." His only leadership is financial. He determines justifications for having affairs, only too happy to have a taste of both worlds. He is one who feigns commitment but it falls short in his adultery, his lack of faithfulness to his wife. His marriage means no commitment to Brenda or anyone outside his marriage. He is selfish and has no respect for the Sabbath nor the covenant of marriage.

Joycelyn—"One who started out as a star until 'rape' stole her innocence and dreams." Deserted by her father, neglected by a drugged out mother and drunken uncle. Left to fend for herself. The result: the mother without a husband, a school dropout. The children have different fathers; she is often looked over, not catered to because she is not status quo.

Uncle Ben –"A 38 year old drunk and disabled veteran." His communion is with a bottle and friends with no morals-cards, drinking, etc.,-Mt. Sherman is only three blocks away. How many churches are near Uncle Ben? Imagine a twenty-three year old who loses an arm in a war where victory was never claimed. His experiences so traumatic until his only solace is in the bottle. He is only accepted by those who are "outsiders" like him.

Mae Jimerson—"A stripper at a local bar." A typical end for a 'problem' foster child. Once rescued from a path of destruction by a Christian family. Tragedy veered her in a direction that threatens to steal her very soul.

Mama Foster/aka Mama Mimi—"A life modeled." She is not just a church person; she is a child of God who is a hearer as well as a doer. The peace established on the true cornerstone after true conversion. The word of God is read in her home on a daily basis. Songs and praises to Him are daily in her home.

James Fieldman—One with "much learning" but never coming into the "knowledge." The prayers of the wife sanctify the husband. The cliché, "behind every good man, there is a good woman" is true. James was a "good" unsaved man. His spiritual paths were formed by his commitment to his wife, Dorothy. He trusted and loved her deeply. His feelings for God were simply the fumes generated off of his love for his wife. He served them both. His reason for everything died on the day that Dorothy died. A Doctorate in Theology with no fear of God? He had no wisdom for "the fear of God is the beginning of wisdom." He was turned over to himself; a reprobated mind.

Bro. Bernard and his father, Bro. Benny—"Strength manifested in the physical" to show how the talents bestowed can be used to conquer evil. The key to their strength is their relationship with God and their prayers and confidence in God.

Cedric—"Young man" who feels like he is somebody through a relationship with a stripper and her boyfriend. He seeks to fit in and bites off more than he planned on chewing; anyone who chooses to be a friend to the world becomes an enemy of God-James 4:4.

Reginald Garrett—"Betrayed by a wife" he loved and respected. He was disillusion by the "faith" after seeing his wife in the arms of another man in Reginald's house, in his bed. A Christian woman whose credibility was shot and held as a marred banner for all "so called" Christian women. Reginald went from a free, respected citizen and husband to an ex-convict, jobless and unwanted by society.

Lisa Garrett—One whose desire for the forbidden leads to two marriages torn apart. The example of one who "does what feels good at the time" with no regard to the consequences. Physical, emotional, and social scars leaves her ridden by "guilt and condemnation."

# Work Cited

*Jacobson, Jim. "The Growing Persecuted Church in Indonesia."18March2008<http://www.lausanneworldpulse.c om/worldreports/79/11-2005>